THE CAGED GRIFFIN

Richard Dungworth

BANTAM BOOKS

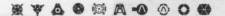

ARMOURON: THE CAGED GRIFFIN
A BANTAM BOOK 978 0 553 82196 3

First published in Great Britain by Bantam Books,
an imprint of Random House Children's Books
A Random House Group Company

Bantam edition published 2010

1 3 5 7 9 10 8 6 4 2

The Random House Group Limited supports the Forest Stewardship
Council (FSC), the leading international forest certification organization.
All our titles that are printed on Greenpeace-approved FSC-certified paper
carry the FSC logo. Our paper procurement policy can be found at
www.rbooks.co.uk/environment.

Mixed Sources
Product group from well-managed
forests and other controlled sources
www.fsc.org   Cert no. TT-COC-2139
© 1996 Forest Stewardship Council
FSC

Set in Palatino

Bantam Books are published by Random House Children's Books,
61–63 Uxbridge Road, London W5 5SA

www.**kids**atrandomhouse.co.uk
www.**rbooks**.co.uk

Addresses for companies within The Random House Group Limited
can be found at: www.randomhouse.co.uk/offices.htm

THE RANDOM HOUSE GROUP Limited Reg. No. 954009

A CIP catalogue record for this book is available from the British Library.

Printed in the UK by CPI Bookmarque, Croydon, CR0 4TD

Far back in the mists of time, an order of warrior knights was forged. They were the Armouron: a dozen heroes dedicated to the ideals of honour and justice. And twelve totems of great power, each borne in the breastplate of an Armouron's suit, were crafted by these First Knights.

The order grew steadily in strength and number. The knowledge, skills and experience of one generation of knights passed to the next.

For millennia, the Armouron campaigned against corruption. But the order came under threat. Giant corporations fought to seize the balance of galactic power. In the struggle to oppose them, all but a handful of Armouron were killed. The survivors were scattered across space.

Now the galaxy has fallen on dark days. Many worlds, including Earth, have been overrun by the largest of the power-hungry corporations. Perfect Corp, led by the sinister Chairman, controls every aspect of life on Earth.

Hope still burns, however, in the Armouron medallions. Many are lost. But five of the original Twelve have found their way into the hands of a group of youngsters, living in the city of Nu-Topia, at the very heart of the Chairman's corrupt regime.

A new generation of Armouron Knights . . .

The new generation of the Armouron

Rake
Armouron title: Templer, the Fearless
Role: Strategy and Offence

Tea-Leaf
Armouron title: Balista, the Shadow
Role: Spy and Scout

Oddball
Armouron title: Sappar, the Inventive
Role: Scavenger and Engineer

Hoax
Armouron title: False-Light, the Trickster
Role: Deception and Misdirection

Snow
Armouron title: Alida, the Shieldmaiden
Role: Protection and Evasion

The Armouron master
Salt

Armouron title: Claymore

Role: Master Craftsman and Teacher

The Armouron Code:

Honour, Duty, Compassion and Justice

1. Perfect Corporation
2. Gladiator Arena
3. Salt's Workshop
4. Armouron Academy
5. Old School
6. SeeBlock Tower
7. Perfect Vision HQ
8. Nu-Topia Hospital
9. Shopping Mall
10. Peace Keeps
11. Fuel Dumps
12. The Park
13. Waste Dumps
14. Epsilon Power Station
15. Spaceport

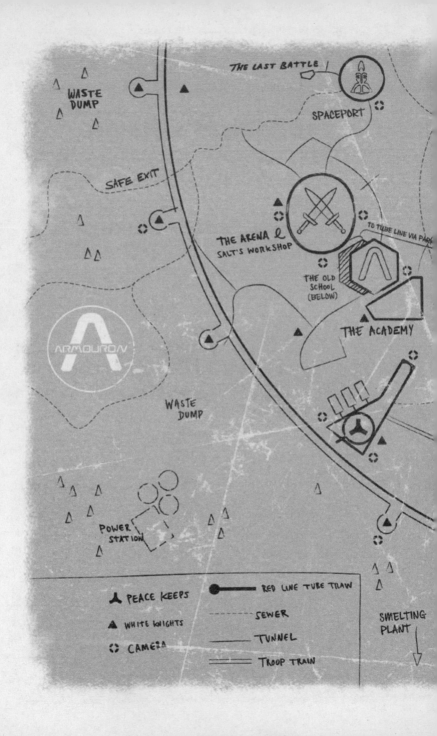

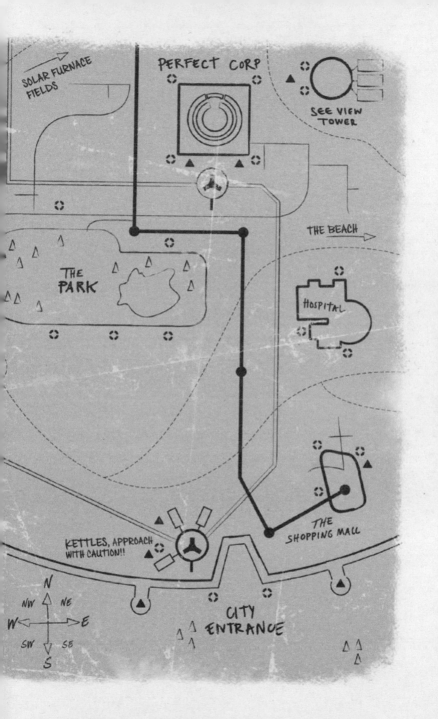

THE CAGED GRIFFIN

Chapter 1
Bruisers and Losers

'Get a move on, you idiot!'

Stamper gave the black-haired boy crouching at his feet an impatient cuff around the head.

'I need to be ready to fight *now*, not in a week's time!'

The boy's shoulders tensed beneath his tunic. He was struggling to keep his temper.

What wouldn't I give to smack him one in his ugly mug, thought Rake bitterly. He snapped shut the last magna-buckle on Stamper's left leg guard. *Half a season in the Arena and he thinks he's it . . .*

He reached for the matching greave lying beside him – the final part of Stamper's armour.

If you can call it that. Rake turned the leg guard over in his hands. Compared to his own unique body armour – which right now was safely stowed in its hiding place – Stamper's seemed crude and clumsy. This showy stuff was what all the Academy Gladiators wore. It might look flashy, but Rake would take his own ultra-light, ultra-tough suit any day.

'I said, *hurry up*!'

A jab from Stamper's toe-cap brought Rake's mind back to the job in hand. Trying to keep his cool, he fitted the greave against the Gladiator's hefty shin and began fastening its buckles. With the last one done, he stood up.

'About time!' Stamper snarled at him. 'Just my luck to be kitted out by a dunk-head like you and your klutz of a sidekick!'

A pale, flame-haired boy stood beside Rake. He was weighed down with the rest of Stamper's equipment. This included a helmet, a shield and a slingshock – a throwing weapon comprising two heavy balls linked by a length of chain.

The boy responded to Stamper's insult with a cheery grin.

But Rake felt his temper flare again. 'Great

put-down,' he said sarcastically under his breath. 'Calling me and Hoax names must make you feel real tough.'

Stamper lunged forward. His livid face was only centimetres from Rake's.

'Don't get smart with me, *cadet*!' he spat. 'You may *think* you're some sort of big-shot, but until you make Gladiator – if there's any chance a no-hoper like you ever *will* – you're just here to do my dirty work. Understood?'

A hush had fallen across the Attiring Chamber. Half a dozen other Gladiators were getting ready for the day's programme of beast-battling, competitions and one-on-one combat. They each had a pair of cadet attendants to assist them. All had stopped working to watch the promising face-off between Rake and Stamper.

But a moment later the tension was broken by a loud buzz that filled the chamber – the first time signal. On cue, a group of seven low podiums rose smoothly from the chamber floor. Each was brightly lit from underneath.

'You're on, big fella!' beamed Hoax, offering Stamper his equipment.

Stamper held Rake's fiery gaze for another long

second, then pushed him away with a dismissive grunt.

'Later, loser!'

He snatched his helmet from Hoax and put it on. Grasping the slingshock's chain in one heavy fist and his shield in the other, he strode towards the glowing platforms.

Stamper and his fellow Gladiators each mounted a podium. The buzzer sounded for a second time. Seven circular apertures opened in the chamber's

high ceiling. Through the openings, the noise of the excited Arena crowd could be plainly heard.

The glowing podiums began to rise, carrying the Gladiators up towards the Arena above. As they ascended, each fighter struck a commanding pose – chest puffed, chin high, feet planted wide.

Within seconds, they had disappeared from view. The sound of the crowd dropped in volume as the podiums plugged the ceiling holes. Even so, the cadets could still hear the enthusiastic yells, screams and applause that greeted the arrival of the Gladiators.

Rake listened to the excited cheering.

They wouldn't be so impressed if they knew the whole thing was a sham.

Before his enrolment as an Armouron knight, Rake's ambition had been to become the most famous Gladiator the Arena had ever seen. Now he knew that the Gladiators' celebrity was built on a lie. Their fights were fixed.

From here on in, although he still wanted to win every Gladiator medallion he could for competition and achievement, he was going to fight for more than a phoney trophy. He would fight for the Armouron ideals: Honour,

Duty, Compassion and Justice. And maybe one day, the people of Nu-Topia would chant *his* name, as they were now chanting Stamper's . . .

A dig in the ribs from Hoax put a stop to Rake's daydreaming.

'Come on, let's get somewhere we can watch!'

The other attendants were now making their way out of the chamber's main exit. Rake and Hoax quietly headed for a second, smaller passageway. As they did so, they were joined by another cadet – a girl, younger than either of them, with a slight build and striking white hair.

'Hiya, Snow,' whispered Hoax. 'Coming to see the show?'

The girl nodded silently.

'Count me in too!'

All three cadets started at the sound of a voice right behind them. A tanned, wirily built girl of around Rake's age stepped out of the shadows near the chamber wall. Unlike the other three children, she wasn't wearing the standard white tunic of an Academy student.

'Tea-Leaf! What are you doing here?' hissed Rake. 'I thought you were supposed to stay down in the Old School!'

'Yeah, yeah,' said Tea-Leaf. 'But Salt has had me polishing shield studs for about a century now. *Soooo* boring! He's busy in his workshop, so I thought I'd sneak up and grab a front-row seat with you lot.' She dismissed Rake's frown. 'Don't worry! Nobody's seen me but you. Stealth is my thing, remember?' She struck an exaggerated pose and whispered dramatically, 'I'm Balista, the Shadow . . .'

Hoax and Snow grinned, but Rake looked unimpressed.

'I heard Stamper getting stroppy just now,' continued the newcomer. 'He really has got it in for you, hasn't he, Rake?'

'Er, not now, Tea-Leaf,' warned Hoax, sensing the rising flush in his best friend's cheeks.

But Tea-Leaf didn't take the hint.

'I mean, there's no way I'd let him talk to *me* like that.'

The anger that Rake had been bottling up now came flooding out. He confronted Tea-Leaf furiously.

'Is that right? So what would you have done, exactly?' His voice dropped to an angry whisper. 'Used your Armouron training to lay a few moves on him, hmm? Or do you not think there's a teensy chance that doing that might have blown our cover, and that maybe that would have been a bit *stupid*?'

Tea-Leaf had touched a nerve. In truth, using his new skills to take down Stamper was exactly what Rake would have instinctively liked to do. But he was already developing a sense of the responsibility that came with his Armouron role. In joining the order, they had become part of a noble, timeless tradition. Its teachings weren't to be employed lightly, in the heat of a petty squabble.

Tea-Leaf looked taken aback.

'No . . . I didn't mean . . .'

'Good!' snapped Rake. 'Because Salt told us not to draw attention to ourselves, remember? Which is why right now you should be down in the Old School, or hanging out with your precious street-friends, instead of risking—'

'Time out, you two!' protested Hoax. 'If we don't get a move on, we'll miss the start. Come on!'

Rake, still looking heated, turned away from Tea-Leaf and followed his friend down the narrow service passage.

Tea-Leaf raised her eyebrows at Snow.

'Someone's a bit grouchy today, aren't they?'

Snow grinned at her. They set off after the boys along the passageway, one of several that criss-crossed beneath the Arena.

'Pen Four is empty,' said Hoax, as he led the way. 'I checked earlier.'

He ducked down another passage, branching to the left. Before they had gone far, it opened into a large, white-walled chamber. Its smooth floor and ceiling sloped to a wide opening at its upper end, which was blocked by a grille of fizzing blue plasma bars.

The four children scrambled across to the mouth of the chamber and threw themselves down in a row. Like the entrances to the other three beast pens, it was set in the high wall that encircled the Arena's combat area. Through the bars, they had an excellent view of the stadium beyond.

And what a scene it was.

Beyond the high inner wall, endless tiers of seating rose up and back. The vast, sophisticated amphitheatre could hold hundreds of thousands – and for today's competitions, every seat was full. A giant holographic projection hovered above the central fight stage, showing close-ups of the Gladiators.

Directly opposite the children's secret vantage point was another beast pen. Above it, a grand balcony jutted out from the stands.

There was a sudden fanfare of electro-trumpets. A group of a dozen important-looking Corporation officials, flanked by White Knight bodyguards, emerged onto the balcony. They were led by a short, rather plump man with a big false smile on his face.

'Here he comes,' said Rake darkly. 'The universe's number one slimeball . . .'

As the rest of his party came to a halt, the man advanced to the front of the balcony, waving majestically at the vast crowd. He addressed his audience, his voice echoing from the stadium's hi-tech sound system.

'Friends! Nu-Topians! Citizens of our Perfect World!'

His greeting was cheered enthusiastically.

'As Chairman, it is my pleasure to welcome you all to today's Gladiatorial Games! In a moment, our valiant contestants . . .'

He gestured to Stamper and the other Gladiators, who were strutting around the centre of the Arena. The crowd gave another appreciative roar.

'. . . will begin today's much-anticipated third round of the Perfect Corporation Gladiator Cup!'

Yet more cheers.

'But before we proceed to the entertainment . . .' The Chairman's expression became uncharacteristically grave. 'I have an important announcement to make. Some breaking news that concerns us all.'

A hush settled over the crowd.

'General Decimal, my Chief of Peace, has recently informed me of a possible catastrophe in the region outside our city's western quarter. There is a derelict power station situated just beyond the Limits. It dates from the pre-fusion nuclear days of the Old City. Regrettably, it has begun leaking toxic radiation.'

Murmurs of concern rumbled around the giant amphitheatre. The Chairman held up his hand to restore order.

'I have the General's assurance that there is no cause for panic. A task force of four thousand White Knights is now getting ready to deal with the situation. Their job is to secure the disaster area, contain the spread of toxins, and stem the leak itself. The Corporation would, however, ask all citizens to avoid the West One region until further notice.'

His artificial smile returned. He raised his arms theatrically.

'Now – let the Games begin!'

The cheering erupted once more. As the Chairman took his seat, the central holographic projection burst into a blaze of light and colour.

Below the corporate balcony, the plasma bars blocking the mouth of Beast Pen One blinked out. A moment later, a huge, bear-like creature came lumbering from the opening. It had massive forelimbs, three monstrous eye-clusters and jaws lined with lethal fangs.

'A prawlkon!' enthused Hoax. 'Excellent!'

'You have to hand it to the Chairman's lot,' admitted Rake. 'That's one realistic robot.'

The children were well aware that the so-called 'beasts' were as phoney as the rest of the Arena pantomime. The 'wild alien creatures' were in truth built to order, in the same top-secret android-manufacturing plants as the White Knights – the

Corporation's supposedly human police force.

The prawlkon was now advancing on the Gladiators, who had drawn their various weapons in readiness. As the boys eagerly watched the fight unfold, Tea-Leaf spoke quietly to Snow.

'What did you make of all that "catastrophe" stuff? Sounded like a load of dunk to me. I reckon he's up to something.'

Although most of the population of Nu-Topia were happily going about their lives believing everything the Chairman told them, the young Armouron knew better now than to trust what he said.

'What sort of something?' asked Snow.

'Dunno,' admitted Tea-Leaf. 'But if he's mobilizing four thousand Kettles, I'll bet it's for more than just a clean-up operation. Chances are somebody is in for a thumping—'

She broke off as a particularly loud cheer went up. One of the Gladiators had scored a hit. The prawlkon was moving awkwardly, dragging its left hind leg.

Stamper had so far concentrated on dodging the robotic foe. Now he began to twirl his slingshock in slow circles, in preparation for an attack. As its twin weights gathered speed, they crackled with electric charge.

'I wish *he'd* get a thumping,' said Rake bitterly. 'I notice he's waited for someone else to disable the thing before he gets involved. Coward.'

'It'll be programmed to lose the fight, anyway,' said Snow. 'To make Stamper and the others look as good as possible.'

'For sure,' agreed Rake. 'And the one-on-ones will have been fixed as well. There hasn't been a fight for months that wasn't rigged. And of course Golden Boy is in with *all* the right peo—'

He was interrupted by the sudden dramatic arrival of a fifth person. A stocky black teenager burst into the pen from the service passage. He was breathing heavily and his peculiar goggles were a little steamed up.

'Oddball?' said Hoax. 'What's up?'

'I thought . . . I'd find . . . you lot here,' panted the newcomer. 'You'd better get a shift on – Brand is on the warpath. Says all cadets have to report for a dormitory check in the next five minutes. Come on!'

Brand was one of the Academy's strictest supervisors. It didn't pay to keep him waiting.

Besides, they were still wearing their cadet identity belts. It would be all too easy for him to check the belt tracking system to discover their whereabouts.

As they hurried after Oddball, back the way they had come, Hoax spoke encouragingly to Rake.

'Cheer up, mate. What you said about the fight-fixing may be true, but you never know – Stamper might come off worse than you expect.'

Rake recognized a familiar twinkle in his friend's eye. Hoax was famous for his practical joking. Rake gave him a searching look.

'What?' said Hoax innocently.

'What did you do, Hoax?' probed Rake.

'Do? Me?' Hoax looked dismayed. 'Dunno what you mean!' He adopted an expression of earnest concern. 'But you know that sling thingy old Numbskull thinks he's so handy with? Well, I had a good look at it while he was getting ready, and if you ask me, it wouldn't take much for one of those chain links to work itself loose.'

He gave Rake a sly wink.

'And if that thing *were* to come apart while you were twirling it about – well, you could easily end up clobbering yourself in the chops!'

A sudden, agonized howl reached their ears from the Arena. It was immediately followed by an outburst of uproarious laughter from the audience.

A broad grin spread across Hoax's face.

'And imagine how embarrassing *that* would be . . .'

Chapter 2
Decimal's Place

Decimal lightly touched the tip of his right index finger to the control screen. A stream of data flooded up the wires in his arm. The computer chips implanted in his brain fizzed into life.

The downloaded information flashed across Decimal's mind. He could see digital maps; readouts from scanners; data on weapons – everything he wanted to know about the soldiers and military equipment under his command.

The Chief of Peace was pleased. Things were going well. Almost all his White Knights were in position. The last unit was being battle-tuned right now, here in the West One Peace Keep. They would soon be ready to join the attack force, bringing it to its full strength of four thousand robot troops.

All that was needed then was the green light from the Chairman.

If things were going to plan, the Chairman would already have made his announcement. Once the cover story about the reactor leak was in place, the Corporation's 'task force' could go into action.

Decimal twitched his right eyelid. It had a micro-switch beneath it – one of many electronic components that the Chief of Peace had chosen to have surgically added to his body. He was as much machine as human.

The control screen filled with a vidcam image of the battle-zone. It showed the front ranks of White Knights, in precise formation, silently awaiting the order to advance. Just beyond them, a curving wall of green light rose from the ground. It was part of a vast dome of energy that enclosed a large circular area.

Another eyelid-twitch activated the camera's zoom. It closed in on a cluster of derelict buildings at the centre of the enclosed area – the remains of the ancient reactor. Decimal switched the camera to thermal imaging mode. He could make out the heat shadows of several bodies moving among the ruined buildings.

Fools, he thought coldly. *They don't stand a chance. They'll be wiped out.*

The troublemakers had been particularly foolish to hide out within striking distance of a Peace Keep. The Corporation's fort-like Keeps stood at regular intervals all around Nu-Topia's perimeter. The West One stronghold was an ideal command centre for Decimal's operation.

'General. Permission to report.'

Decimal turned to look into the visored face of a White Knight, standing stiffly to attention behind him. The soldier's gleaming armour was marked with a black shoulder flash.

'Yes, Captain? What is it?'

'Sir, the executive shuttle is approaching the Keep's docking bay. Estimated time of arrival less than four minutes, sir.'

'Thank you, Captain.'

So the Chairman was on his way. Good. Now the party could *really* get started . . .

Chapter 3
An Uninvited Guest

Rake flexed the fingers of his armoured gauntlets. He clenched his left fist tightly and felt its gauntlet harden, as its plastallic components locked down. His fist now had the solidity and destructive power of a wrecking ball.

Not for the first time, Rake marvelled at the craftsmanship of his red and black Armouron suit. The sense of power that it gave him was awesome. In a way that he couldn't quite fathom, putting it on seemed to create a connection between himself and the great warriors who had championed the Armouron tradition since the order's foundation, many millennia ago. Suited up like this, he felt invincible.

He grasped the hilt of his shortsword with his right hand and slid it smoothly from its scabbard. Battle-ready, he confronted his waiting opponent.

'You're absolutely sure about this?' Rake's voice was full of concern. 'You want me to come at you full on, no holding back?'

Salt faced Rake with neither weapon nor body armour. He seemed ill-equipped for a bout of combat. Rake knew that the old man could handle himself – he had seen him in the heat of battle. But his own combat skills had been improving fast under Salt's tuition. He was worried about injuring his teacher.

But Salt only gave a wry smile and set his broad body in a defensive stance. He met his student's anxious look with a steady gaze.

'Whenever you're ready, young man.'

Reluctantly, Rake prepared to fight. He cleared his mind of all distracting thoughts, as Salt had instructed. His only focus must be the fight.

If I feint with a sword-jab to his side, he'll have to dodge – then I can catch him with a knockout punch while he's off balance. He was keen to end the bout quickly, so as to inflict minimum harm.

He raised his sword arm and shifted his balance

onto his back foot. Then, with lightning speed, he lunged at Salt . . .

. . . and found himself flat on his back on the training room's cold stone floor.

His chest was pinned beneath one of Salt's heavy knees and the point of his own sword was pressed to his throat.

Salt gave a disapproving grunt. He released his hold, rose to stand over Rake, and hauled him to his feet.

'Still too slow,' he growled, handing back Rake's weapon, hilt first.

As Rake re-sheathed his sword, looking rather crestfallen, Salt reached for the boy's scarlet breastplate. He plucked a small disc from the snap-grab fastening at its centre. Then he turned to address his other pupils.

All four of Rake's fellow Armouron – Hoax, Oddball, Snow and Tea-Leaf – had been

watching him in action. As always, their training session was taking place at night, while the rest of the Academy slept. Since Salt had recruited them, the four cadets had become used to slipping unnoticed from their sleeping quarters, leaving their identity belts beneath their mattresses. They reached the hidden chambers of the Old School through a concealed entrance in Salt's armour workshop. Tea-Leaf used a secret passage from the shuttle garage to sneak into the Academy and join them.

Down here, in the lamp-lit gloom, Salt could instruct them in the lore of the ancient order they had now joined, confident that there was little chance of detection.

The old armourer held up the disc he had taken from Rake's breastplate in his thick fingers.

'Never forget,' he rumbled, 'that as an Armouron Knight, your greatest strength comes from this – your medallion. It is the very source of a knight's power. It holds the knowledge, skill, experience and spirit of all those honoured to bear it before you. Only when you connect with it – when you feel and channel the Flow – can you fulfil your own potential.'

He turned to Rake.

'Templer, you are fortunate to bear a medallion worn by one of the Twelve, the first and greatest of the Armouron. If you learn to harness its formidable power, you may yet become a worthy knight. Fail to do so and you will for ever remain lowly enough to be easily overcome by an unarmed old man.'

Salt handed the medallion to Rake, who meekly snapped it back in place.

'Now – someone else give it a try.' Salt nodded to Tea-Leaf. She looked a little taken aback.

'You want *me* to attack you?'

'No. I want you to attempt to channel the unique powers of *your* medallion. It can greatly add to your talents as a spy or scout. It will give your suit unequalled qualities of stealth and all your senses will be heightened.'

'I thought our helmet visors did that, anyway?' Hoax piped up.

'Your visors allow you to see through cloaking shields and other optical deceptions,' acknowledged Salt. 'But with the help of her medallion, Balista's sensory abilities will go far beyond that.'

He turned his attention back to Tea-Leaf.

'See what you can do. Close your eyes and focus your other senses. Your medallion will enhance them, if you can calm your mind and channel its Flow.'

'OK.' Tea-Leaf sounded less than confident. 'I'll give it a go.'

She shut her eyes, took a deep breath, then slowly exhaled.

After several seconds of silence, Salt spoke softly.

'Now, tell me what you sense – what you can see in your mind's eye.'

'It's a bit weird,' mumbled Tea-Leaf. 'I can just about make out each of you, like hints of colour against black. It's not very clear, though . . .'

'It will become more so in time,' said Salt.

'And . . . well . . . I can sort of *feel* the basic shape of the room – where the walls and doors are . . .'

'Good.'

'There's something else too.' Tea-Leaf screwed her eyes even more tightly shut in concentration. 'Something small and mobile, a tiny grey blur. It's moving about in the air – too fast to track . . .'

Salt's expression suddenly darkened. 'A grey

aura signifies deception – something cloaked.' He scanned the training room with an anxious gaze.

Thinking fast, Snow quickly slipped her helmet over her head and dropped its visor. She too scanned the room frantically. Moments later, she cried out.

'She's right! There's some sort of shiny flying thing hovering just—'

A sudden *twang-phizzz-thud* cut her off. Something sliced through the air and buried itself in the far wall of the chamber. A golden object, the size of a small bird, appeared out of thin air just above Rake's shoulder. It dropped like a stone to clatter onto the floor.

Rake turned to see what had just shot narrowly past his head. He stared wide-eyed at the crossbow bolt embedded in the stone wall.

'Sorry!' murmured Tea-Leaf. She lowered her bow, looking rather shocked at her own spur-of-the-moment action. 'It's just that . . . well . . . everything sort of came into clear focus for a split-second and I could see it was right behind you, Rake . . . and what with you saying that about deception, master, I thought whatever it was might be dangerous—'

'*Dangerous!*' hissed Rake. His face was drained of colour. 'Did you not think that shooting past me was maybe a bit *dangerous* too? What if you'd—'

'Enough, Rake!' barked Salt. 'Tea-Leaf acted on instinct, to protect you.' He turned to Tea-Leaf sternly. 'It *was* rash to take such a risky shot . . .'

Tea-Leaf looked down.

'. . . but your aim is to be commended,' continued Salt, more warmly. 'As is your success in harnessing the Flow. A worthy effort.'

'What is that thing?' asked Hoax. Oddball had crouched over the mysterious golden object and was examining it cautiously. He lifted it onto his palm and rose to his feet. The others gathered round to take a closer look.

It was a mechanical creature – a replica of a giant beetle, crafted from brass and copper. Its wing cases were engraved with swirling geometric patterns. One was badly dented where Tea-Leaf's crossbow bolt had glanced off it. Its delicate wings, made from ultra-fine copper leaf, were trapped awkwardly, still flicking weakly.

'Some sort of surveillance device, I fear,' said Salt. 'A mechanical spy. Though from its design, I don't think this was made by the Corporation.'

He spoke earnestly to Oddball.

'I need you to find out exactly what this thing is, and where it came from.' Salt's brow furrowed. 'It may already have recorded or transmitted the details of our training session. If so, we need to know.'

'I'm on it, master,' replied Oddball. He laid the still-twitching beetle device carefully on its back on the floor. Then he flipped open one of his suit's yellow chest panels and took out a micro-toolkit and folding pair of telescopic goggles. 'Stripping down this little beauty will be a pleasure.'

Salt addressed the other four young knights.

'In the circumstances, I think it best to abandon tonight's training. We'll regroup when Oddball has something to report. In the meantime, be vigilant. Take extra care not to expose yourselves to suspicion.'

'A clack lot of good that'll do,' muttered Hoax to Rake, as the two boys began removing their armour a piece at a time, 'if our cover's already blown.'

'Let's just hope it isn't, Hoax.' Rake looked grave. 'For all our sakes.'

Chapter 4
Message in a Beetle

'. . . and this morning's top news once more,' drawled the holovid newsreader. 'Following yesterday's discovery of a toxic leak at the derelict Epsilon power station, the Board of Directors has announced that an exclusion zone has been set up around the reactor. Members of the public will not be allowed within three kilometres of the site. In a statement last night, the Chairman said that this measure was one of several being taken by Perfect Corp to ensure the continued safety of Nu-Topia's citizens.'

Hoax looked up from his bowl of lukewarm nutri-gruel and gave a snort.

'Safety, my backside! He's up to something out there on the Limits, or I'm a Venusian.'

Rake took a final reluctant mouthful from his own bowl of grey gloop, then shoved it away in disgust.

'Certainly smells a bit fishy, doesn't it?'

'What?' smirked Hoax. 'The leak story or your porridge?'

Snow sat opposite the two boys on one of the long benches of the Academy canteen. The hall was warm and airless, and filled with the chatter of the many cadets and Gladiators who lined its tables. For anyone who had had very little sleep – like the three young Armouron – it was an unpleasant atmosphere. The mornings after their secret night-time training sessions were always a struggle.

The news update was being projected in the centre of each table. The three friends watched bleary-eyed as the bulletin continued. The familiar face of the Chairman suddenly occupied the space before them.

'The situation, though serious, has been brought under control by the swift and courageous action of our White Knight task force . . .'

'Kettles can't be courageous,' grumbled Hoax. 'They're androids.'

'*We* know that,' said Rake. 'But the rest of Nu-Topia still buy the Corporation's line – that they're "elite human troops". They'll be cheering them on too.'

Hoax shook his head despairingly.

'. . . *under General Decimal's direction,*' oozed the Corporation boss, '*a state-of-the-art containment field – an electromagnetic barrier – has been set up around the danger area. Nothing can pass through it. The handling of this crisis once again shows that under Perfect Corporation management . . .*'

The Chairman gave his trademark smile.

'. . . *it's a Perfect World.*'

As the holovid winked out, Snow pulled a face.

'Urgh! That man's oilier than canteen custard!'

The boys chuckled their agreement.

'I wonder where Oddball is,' said Rake. 'He never came to bed. Must've been up all night tinkering with that beetle thing.'

'Well, if anyone can figure out what it is, Oddball can,' said Hoax. 'Nobody knows their way round mechanical stuff better than he does.'

'Do you know what I reckon it is?' mused Rake. 'I reckon—'

But the others never heard his theory. At that moment, the tall, thin figure of Brand came striding towards their table, a severe expression on his face.

'Right, you three!' he snapped. 'You're to come with me immediately. Punishment detail!'

A hush fell over the hall as the cadets on the neighbouring tables stopped chattering. They were keen to see what had got Brand fired up.

'Punishment?' asked Rake, puzzled. 'What for?'

The wiry supervisor gave him a nasty look. 'You *know* what for, boy! Master Salt has heard about the little stunt you pulled in the Arena yesterday.'

He nodded to where the Gladiators sat at the top end of the hall. Stamper was watching them with a satisfied sneer on his face – and a very obviously blackened left eye.

'I don't follow,' protested Rake innocently.

Brand leaned towards him.

'Either you or one of your friends here was responsible for tampering with a Gladiator's equipment,' he hissed. 'If it wasn't you, then perhaps you'd care to give me a name . . .'

Rake shrugged.

'Sorry – dunno what the clack you're talking about. I heard Stamper was just so clumsy he whacked himself in the eye.'

Hoax and Snow tried, unsuccessfully, to hide their smirks. Brand's face reddened.

'I imagine the three of you will be less pleased with yourselves once you've spent the next three days engaged in the task Salt has devised as your punishment.' He gave a cruel smile. 'Cleaning out the stinking, rat-infested drainage tunnels in the bowels of our Academy's ancient foundations. No breaks, no meals, no sleep.' His leer widened. 'That *will* be fun, won't it?'

He stepped back and resumed his fierce scowl.

'Now – *move it!*'

Brand was right – the old tunnels really did stink. The part of the Old School where the Armouron met secretly had a pleasantly cool, earthy atmosphere. But this area was altogether different. As Brand marched them along yet another dingy, damp passageway, the cadets wrinkled their noses against the foul smell.

From the shadows up ahead, an opening

appeared in the passageway's wall. Through it, a set of spiralling stone steps descended into darkness.

'Down there!' snapped Brand, giving Rake an impatient shove.

The stairs led to a small, badly lit chamber. There was someone waiting for them in the gloom. It was Salt, stony-faced. Oddball stood beside him, looking decidedly glum.

Salt said nothing by way of greeting, but nodded to Brand as he emerged from the stairwell behind them.

'I found these three at breakfast,' reported the supervisor. 'I see you've already tracked down the other one.'

'Yes. Thank you, Brand,' growled Salt. 'You may leave them to me.' He cast a harsh gaze across the four youngsters. 'As their supervisor, their foolish behaviour has caused me much embarrassment. I wish to oversee their punishment personally.'

Brand looked only too pleased to leave their company for the breathable air of the upper Academy. As the sound of his footfalls faded, Salt relaxed his frown. Oddball's face brightened and he crossed to greet his friends.

✹ ⚐ ⬠ ⬤ ◉ Ⓐ ⬧ ⬢ ⬡ ✾

'Hi, guys. Glad you could make it.'

A moment later, a sixth figure emerged from a shadowy corner of the chamber. It was Tea-Leaf.

Rake looked puzzled. 'What's going on, master?'

'Apologies for the necessary deception,' rumbled Salt, 'and for our rather . . . *fragrant* surroundings. I needed a way to get you away from your ordinary duties – and from general company – without raising suspicion.'

'That's OK, master,' said Hoax. 'When Brand said he was acting on your behalf, we kind of figured you were up to something. But how did you know about the Stamper thing?'

Salt raised an eyebrow.

'Your childish pranks are the subject of much admiring gossip among your fellow cadets, young man.'

Hoax looked rather pleased with himself.

'So why the cover story?' quizzed Rake. 'What's up?'

Salt looked meaningfully at Oddball, who took his cue. He reached into his tunic pocket and took out the replica beetle.

'I spent most of last night taking our little bug

friend here to pieces, then assembling it again. I've never seen anything like it,' enthused the gadget-mad cadet. 'It's a mechanical masterpiece.'

He released a catch on the beetle's underside and its wing cases swung open to reveal its inner workings. They were incredibly complex – a mass of tiny interlocking cogs, gears, microscopic levers, cams and cranks. Every square millimetre of the casing was crammed with miniature mechanical components.

'The whole thing – flight mechanism, navigation system, everything – is mechanical. Sophisticated clockwork, powered by an ultra-efficient coil-spring. And it has a cloaking device created by

🕸 🔱 🔺 ⊛ 🔯 🅰 ⬠ ◈ ⬡ ⬢

a clever combination of lenses and mirrors in its casing. There are no electrical components – so its activity won't show up on any of the Corporation's tracking systems.'

As his fellow Armouron peered at the beetle's intricate insides, Oddball continued.

'And it's *not* a surveillance device. There's no spying kit – no recording or transmitting apparatus. Just this tiny payload compartment.' He used the tip of his little finger to point to a small silver cube. 'This thing is a clockwork courier. It was set up to find its way to the Old School and deliver something.'

He pulled a slim metal rod from behind his goggles and used it to expertly prod another catch inside the beetle. There was a soft *click* and the top of the silver cube sprang open. Oddball tipped the bug over and something yellow, the size of a pea, dropped onto his palm.

'This, to be precise,' said Oddball. He held up the object for his audience to admire. It was a small, multi-faceted, semi-transparent stone.

'It's beautiful!' gasped Snow.

'But why would anyone want to secretly send you – or us – a gemstone?' Rake asked Salt.

'It's not a gemstone,' replied his tutor. He plucked the yellow object from Oddball's palm and looked at it closely. 'Watch.'

He approached one of the small oil lamps by which the chamber was lit. After scrutinizing the crystal-like stone for a few more moments, he held it close to the lamp.

As the lamplight passed through the stone, it was refracted by the prism's angled surfaces. The beam spread, to be projected onto the wall of the chamber. Parts of it were more intense, creating flickering golden lines on the wall.

Snow was the first to realize what she was seeing.

'They're letters!'

It was true. All five children could now make out the flickering message:

CAGED IN EPSILON
HAVE WINGS
NEED DOOR
GRIFFIN

'It's a message prism,' said Salt. 'An ancient technique. Words are inscribed in miniature on the prism. They're only revealed when light is shone through the correct face.'

'Epsilon . . .' murmured Rake. 'That's the leaking reactor, isn't it?'

Salt nodded. 'Only I suspect that in reality there's no leak. Judging by this, the Chairman is using his containment field to isolate an enemy, not dangerous radiation. Evidently, he doesn't want the general public to know what he's up to.'

'No change there, then,' put in Hoax.

'So whoever sent this is "caged in Epsilon" . . .' said Snow, 'and wants us to create a "door" – an escape route, do you think?'

Salt nodded again.

'That seems the most probable interpretation. And judging by the "have wings" phrase, I think it likely that the party in question has a ship at their disposal.'

'But what about the "griffin" bit?' puzzled Snow. 'What's that about?'

Tea-Leaf, who had been silent so far, now spoke.

'It's a name,' she said softly.

The others looked at her enquiringly.

'I remember it from my childhood, on the streets.' She seemed uncomfortable discussing her past. 'Most of the time I had to look out for myself. But when I was really little, there was this old man. A street-dweller, like me. He wasn't around all the time or anything. But when things got bad – when I got ill or really hungry – he'd almost always turn up. He'd bring me food, or dry clothes. And he'd tell me stories. A lot of them were about a man called Griffin.'

Salt watched Tea-Leaf thoughtfully, as she continued.

'He said Griffin was a freedom fighter, a sworn enemy of the Corporation. He thought a great deal of him. I can remember him saying that he valued Griffin's life as highly as his own.'

'He was right about him being the Chairman's enemy,' said Salt.

It was his turn to be the focus of five inquisitive stares.

'I know something of a "Griffin" too,' he explained. 'It was the Gladiator name of one of my first pupils here at the Academy. A talented fighter and a decent man – and one of only a handful of people who would know they could reach me in the Old School.'

'So he's a friend of yours?' asked Rake.

'*Was* a friend,' corrected Salt. 'When the Corporation began to "arrange" more and more of the Arena results, Griffin spoke out against the fight-fixing. The Chairman couldn't allow that.' The old man's tone was bitter. 'Griffin vanished one night. Tonight is the first time I've heard his name in nearly ten years.'

He addressed Tea-Leaf.

'Do you know where your street friend is now? Perhaps he could tell us more.'

Tea-Leaf shook her head.

'It's ages since I last saw him. He came to see me on my tenth birthday. Not that I'm really sure when my birthday is . . .'

Tea-Leaf looked down awkwardly for a moment, before continuing.

'But I have heard Griffin's name crop up more recently. There's been a lot of street-talk about anti-Corporation activity on the outskirts. The word is that there's an organized band of Skirters, based just beyond the Limits. They've been causing the White Knights a dunk-load of trouble. They've staged raids against some of the main power-generating facilities – like the solar furnace fields northeast of the city. And the rumours mention a leader: Griffin.'

Rake turned to Salt again. 'So, let's say your ex-Gladiator pal and his Skirter friends are being held inside the containment field and that they've somehow managed to get this beetle thing to bring us a cry for help,' he summed up. 'What do we do now?'

'Do?' growled Salt, raising his heavy brows. 'I should have thought that was obvious. We get them out of there.'

His forehead creased once more in a frown.

'The real question, my young friend, is *how* . . .'

Chapter 5
Model Army

'Very impressive, General Decimal,' murmured the Chairman. 'Very impressive indeed.'

He was standing beside his Chief of Peace on the gallery of the West One Peace Keep's main control room. A holographic scale model of the battle-zone stretched out below him. At its centre he could clearly see the old Epsilon reactor. The surrounding area was entirely enclosed by a translucent green dome – the containment field. All around its outside stood ranks of miniature white figures, each labelled with a tiny red identity code.

The ring of White Knights had only one gap. Decimal had just explained to his superior that the final unit of androids was making its way into position. In fact, there they were – a perfect block of tiny white troops marching west across the display.

'Of course, it would have been much simpler just to have blitzed the place,' observed the Chairman. 'Taken out the whole site with a Flying Fortress airstrike.'

'Indeed, sir,' agreed Decimal. 'I estimate a single kiloton F-bomb would have left no survivors.'

'But we can't have people thinking that the Perfect Corporation governs by brute force, eh? There's no surer way to create public support for these irritating Skirter fools than by making martyrs of them.'

Skirters weren't a new problem. Ever since the Chairman had taken control of Nu-Topia, there had been those who opposed him. He had seen to it that most disappeared permanently, or were locked up in one of the Corporation's underground detention centres. The lucky ones fled the city.

But they tended not to go far. The wastelands that surrounded Nu-Topia were uninhabitable, even for an outlaw. It was a long way to any other settlement and few welcomed outsiders. Most exiles tried to survive on the outskirts, just beyond the Limits. Here, they could scavenge in the Dumps – the mountainous waste heaps that encircled the city.

In the past, the Skirters had lacked the leadership to be any real threat. The White Knights had easily dealt with the occasional badly planned raid. But over the last year, a small, well-organized group of exiles had staged a series of successful attacks on Corporation facilities. They had become a serious thorn in the Chairman's side.

But not for much longer.

The Chairman looked across the battle-zone model spread before him. The miniature troops looked like so many thousand toy soldiers. But in reality, he knew, each one of them was a remorseless, ultra-efficient killing machine. When they advanced – soon, now – nothing within the field would be left alive.

'The future looks a little grim for our Skirter friends, wouldn't you say, General?' sneered the Chairman.

'Without a doubt, sir.' Decimal attempted a smile – an expression which really didn't suit him.

'By my calculations our Knights outnumber them by at least eighty to one.'

'Excellent!' The Chairman's cruel grin widened. 'As you know, my old friend, there's nothing I dislike more than a fair fight . . .'

Chapter 6
Tactics and Tactlessness

'So – let's run through it one more time,' said Salt. 'Just to make sure everyone is clear on their role. You first, Alida.'

The old armourer and his five students were still gathered in the foul-smelling chamber in the depths of the Academy. But now the children were fully clad in their Armouron suits and clutching their helmets. Four cadet identity belts lay in a pile in one corner of the chamber.

Their transformation was far more than just a superficial change of outfit. In removing their belts and donning their armour, the cadets had shed their day-to-day characters and adopted the mindset of the knight warrior. Salt took in their purposeful expressions approvingly. They looked worthy of their titles: Templer, the Fearless; Balista, the Shadow; False-Light, the Trickster; Sappar, the Inventive; and young Alida, the Shieldmaiden.

'Rake, Tea-Leaf and I are responsible for taking out the containment field,' began Snow. 'We're to find our way inside the field generator, without being detected, and disable the control system.'

'But just so *part* of the field fails,' chipped in Rake. 'Not the whole shebang. And only temporarily too – for around a minute or so.'

'Good,' rumbled Salt. 'The field is actually a geodesic dome – that means it is made up of lots of small triangular shield zones. If you can knock out just one of those zones, it should provide Griffin with the "door" he needs. And they won't know it is sabotage.'

'You're hoping they'll put it down to a technical glitch?' asked Hoax.

Salt nodded gravely. 'We must do everything we can to carry out this operation undetected. If the Chairman suspects foul play – particularly Armouron involvement – things will quickly turn nasty.'

He turned to Hoax and Oddball.

'And you two?'

'Me and Oddball are the contact team,' began Hoax. 'It's our job to find our way to the Skirter base and tell Griffin when and where the containment field is going to fail. Then they can be ready and waiting when their chance comes to make a break for it.'

'We get around the problem of not being able to go through the containment field by going *under* it,' expanded Oddball. 'Through the disused sewer system.'

Salt nodded again. 'Fortunately, the abandoned system goes out far beyond the current Limits, from the days when it served the entire Old City. Its tunnels will take you right underneath the Epsilon site. And they can be accessed from the Old School drains – hence our current location . . .'

'I get the bit about going under the field,' said Hoax. 'But how will we know where to find Griffin once we surface inside it? Judging by the news shots we saw, the isolated area is pretty big.'

'No problem,' said Oddball confidently. He slid open a panel in his leg armour and took out the clockwork courier beetle. 'It was easy enough to work out the original departure coordinates of this little beauty from the way its navigation mechanism was set up. If we head for that location, we should end up smack bang in the middle of the Skirter camp.'

'Why can't we just use the beetle to get a message to Griffin?' asked Tea-Leaf. 'It must have found a way past the containment field on its way here.'

'We probably could have – if you hadn't shot it,' replied Oddball. 'I could reset the mechanism to retrace its route, at a push. But some of the tiny bubble-valves that control its flight direction are damaged. The optical cloaking is a bit of a mess too. It would take me a fair bit of time to fix.'

'Time we don't have,' said Salt. 'Besides, your role is more than just as message-bearers. Your suits and skills will allow you to assist Griffin's people in other ways, I hope.'

Tea-Leaf seemed satisfied. But Snow too had a query.

'Master,' she said quietly. 'Why do we need to risk taking out the field at all? Wouldn't it be simpler for Griffin and his people to follow Hoax and Oddball back through the sewers?'

'A good question, Alida,' replied Salt. 'But I think we can assume that for these individuals, an escape back into the city would be no escape at all. If they return, the Corporation will not rest until it has hunted them down. If Griffin has gone to the trouble of acquiring a ship of some kind, it must be because he feels unable to dodge the authorities any longer. We must help him and his friends get well clear of Nu-Topia.'

He paused.

'Any more questions?'

Rake cleared his throat a little awkwardly. 'With respect, master,' he began, 'do you think it's wise for *all* of us to be involved? I mean . . . it sounds like a pretty risky assignment, and some of us' – his gaze fell fleetingly on Tea-Leaf – 'have had hardly any training . . .'

Tea-Leaf's cheeks coloured.

'If you mean you don't trust me not to mess things up, why don't you just say so?'

'It's not about trust,' argued Rake, avoiding her fiery glare. 'It's just . . . well, to be honest, you're still new to all this, aren't you? The rest of us have had years of Academy training. And you're not exactly the best at controlling your impulses. Look what happened last night – you nearly took my head off with that crossbow shot!'

'I'm beginning to wish I had,' snapped Tea-Leaf. Hoax failed to hide a snigger.

Rake's tone became less gentle. 'One reckless move like that under pressure and you could blow the whole mission! At the moment, you're a loose cannon. I don't want to find myself staring down a Kettle's laser barrel because a hot-headed rookie—'

'*Enough*!'

It was very rare for Salt to raise his voice. Rake fell instantly silent in the face of the old man's formidable anger.

'The armour in which you are fortunate enough to stand before me was crafted for champions of the Armouron ideals: Honour, Duty, Compassion and Justice!' thundered Salt. '*Not* for a bunch of bickering infants!'

He glared at Rake.

'You, my lad, will respect *my* judgement as to who is, or is not, fit for field operations. Balista is your comrade at arms and deserves your loyalty and respect, not your criticism. Or have you forgotten our code of honour? *Stand Together, Battle as One!*'

He turned away from the humbled teenager.

'And you, young lady—'

But Tea-Leaf had vanished. The space beside Snow, where she had been standing only seconds earlier, was vacant.

Oddball looked totally bewildered. 'Where'd she go? She can't just *disappear* like that . . .'

Salt's brow creased in a frown.

'You forget – Balista's medallion and the suit I crafted for her greatly increase her talents for disguise. If she chose to slip away, it is well within her powers.'

'You shouldn't have upset her, Rake!' chided Snow.

'You were a bit over the top, mate,' agreed Hoax.

Rake said nothing, but looked down uncomfortably.

'We don't have time for this!' growled Salt. 'If we don't act immediately, Griffin and his people are as good as dead. The last thing we need is one of our team, fully suited, going walkabout!'

He fell silent for a few seconds. Moments later,

he had regained his usual composure.

'We must focus on our main goal,' he said decisively. 'I want the four of you to go ahead with the mission as planned, setting off immediately. I'll try to track down Balista and get her back onside.'

The four young knights nodded earnestly. They quickly slipped on their helmets, snap-locking them in place.

As Salt watched them hurry away in their pairs, he muttered anxiously to himself.

'I only hope I find her before anyone else does . . .'

Chapter 7
The Chairman's Sister

Tea-Leaf had vanished.

Salt had combed the entire Old School, but there was no sign of her. Now he was back in the upper Academy, hurrying along the corridor from his workshop. He knew that Tea-Leaf had found her way into the Attiring Chamber yesterday. Today, it would be out of use. Maybe he would find her lying low there, feeling sorry for herself.

I wish I hadn't done such a good job on that suit of hers, thought the old armourer bitterly. He had put great care and skill into crafting Tea-Leaf's armour so that it would maximize her ability to conceal herself. He had never imagined that *he* would be first person to test its effectiveness.

As long as she hasn't gone far . . .

His fear was that in a fit of temper, Tea-Leaf might do something rash. She was a great kid and talented too. He was confident that he – and her medallion – had chosen well. But there was some truth in what Rake had said. She *was* rather more unpredictable than Salt would have liked.

He could talk to her about that when he found her. The priority was to get her back. While she was missing, in full armour, she was in danger of blowing her own cover, and possibly the whole team's.

As he rounded a bend in the corridor, Salt nearly charged headlong into a tall, athletically built woman coming the other way.

'Look where you're going, old-timer!' she snapped. 'Why the rush?'

Salt's heart sank. This was the last person he needed to run into.

The woman now glaring at him was the older sister of the Chairman himself. Her influence within the Corporation was second only to that of her baby brother. She was also the most famous of all the Arena's stars – a fearsome fighter, who had cut down opponent after opponent with her cruelly curved, laser-edged ion-sica. She had been beaten only once in her long career, by the very man Salt's Armouron team was now trying to rescue – Griffin.

This dangerous, ambitious, scheming woman was known solely by her Gladiator name: *Lanista*. It was from ancient Eurolese and loosely meant 'she who commands others'. It fitted her well.

'Well, whatever your business, it will have to wait,' she told Salt haughtily. 'Strangely enough, I was actually on my way to see *you*.'

She was carrying a pair of shoulder guards. She thrust them against Salt's broad chest, so that he had no choice but to take hold of them.

'My spaulders. That fool Brand made them. They're useless.'

Salt remained silent.

'They restrict my movement when I raise my arms,' continued Lanista. 'I want them fixed as a matter of priority.'

When Salt still failed to respond, the Chairman's sister grew impatient. She was used to immediate obedience from her inferiors.

'Let me spell it out.' She took hold of the armourer's shoulders and turned him forcibly round. 'You go back to your grimy little workshop now. You don't leave till my armour works like it should. The moment it's fixed, you bring it to me. I'll be at Corporation Headquarters for the rest of the day. Understood?' She gave Salt a condescending smile. 'Or is that too complicated for your prehistoric brain?'

Inside his head, Salt was screaming with frustration.

I don't have time for this! I need to find Tea-Leaf! What about the mission?

But there was nothing to be done. He couldn't afford to risk going against Lanista's wishes. It was only likely to raise her suspicions.

He nodded respectfully.

'I understand, madam. I'll see to it immediately.'

Clutching the offending shoulder guards, he hurried back the way he had come.

Less than an hour later, Lanista was striding along a very different passageway. It led to the boardroom of Perfect Corporation's headquarters. The impressive HQ building was in downtown Nu-Topia, not far from the Academy. It was the dark

🟊 ⚙ 🔺 ⦿ ◎ 🅰 🔺 ⬡ ⬡ ⬢

heart of the Chairman's corrupt organization.

Lanista reached the entrance to the boardroom and impatiently wiped a finger over its DNA-recognition pad. The double doors sliced open, admitting her to the spacious, luxurious office beyond.

The room was dominated by a large black table, surrounded by twelve high-backed chairs. Right now, they were empty, and the office deserted.

At the table's far end – where Lanista herself always sat – part of its glossy surface was blinking with a red glow. A message.

She crossed to lay her palm on the flashing area. A miniature projection of her brother instantly appeared above the tabletop.

'Hi, Big Sis,' grinned the mini-Chairman. 'Sorry not to be around. I've popped out of the office to meet up with Decimal. We're all set to begin clearing up our little problem at the Epsilon site.'

Clearing up our little problem. Lanista smiled to herself. Her brother had a tendency to make the use of lethal force sound like everyday tidying up.

'By the way,' the message continued, 'from the scans he's taken, Decimal thinks it's very likely that your old friend Griffin *is* leading the Skirter group. Just as you suspected. I'll try to bring you back a souvenir of his death. In the meantime, hold the fort while I'm gone. Ciao!'

As the hologram cut out, Lanista heard footsteps behind her. She turned to see a man in a black uniform enter the room.

'Director, I have a report for the Chairman, from the DEM.'

The DEM – the Department for Energy Management – was responsible for checking the use of electricity and computer data by Nu-Topia's citizens. Some years ago, the Chairman had banned any unauthorized use of electrical power or digital information. You now needed Corporation permission to run any electric device, or even send an email. The Chairman had claimed this was in the public interest. Energy was scarce, he argued, and its use needed to be controlled. In reality, it gave him a stranglehold on the city.

'My brother isn't here,' Lanista told the messenger. 'You may deliver your report to me.'

The man bowed his head respectfully.

'Our SeeBlock scanners have recently picked

up two instances of unauthorized power usage, Director.'

The SeeBlock tower, which loomed over central Nu-Topia, was the DEM's centre of surveillance.

'Fascinating,' said Lanista dryly. 'And why, exactly, is that a matter for the Board?'

The man in black was looking increasingly nervous.

'The location of the surges is unusual, Director. Both occurred underground, in the disused sewer tunnels.'

Now Lanista was interested.

'Go on.'

The man hurriedly produced a slim display screen, showing a computerized map.

'The first trace was here – directly beneath sector W14. The second, fifty-seven minutes later, was in sector W26.' Two small blips blinked on the display. 'This suggests that the party responsible is moving along this tunnel section.'

'And if they carried on in that direction? Do we have an idea of their possible destination?'

'Their projected course leads out towards the West One area, Director.'

And if they continued beyond that, thought Lanista,

studying the diagram, *they'd pass right underneath the Epsilon site . . .*

This was too much of a coincidence. Someone was secretly making their way directly towards where Griffin was holed up. It had to be some form of rescue attempt.

A thin smile spread across Lanista's face.

And if I follow, they'll lead me right to him.

'Captain, I want a squad of Knights at my disposal within the next five minutes, fully equipped for underground exploration.'

'Yes, Director.' The man turned and hurried away.

'Whoever it is sneaking around down there,' murmured the Chairman's sister to herself, 'I think it's time I paid them a surprise visit . . .'

Chapter 8
Pest Control

Things were not turning out quite as Hoax had imagined. Being involved in the daring rescue of a band of rebel fighters *sounded* pretty exciting. But as he waded slowly through the thick, grey sludge that slopped around his knees, and peered ahead along the murky sewer tunnel, Hoax felt that the reality was so far proving rather less thrilling.

Oddball, striding through the unpleasant gunk beside him, gave a sudden groan of dismay.

'What *now*?'

A little way ahead, the tunnel appeared to be blocked. Hoax squinted through his helmet visor's night-sight overlay. Given that it was completely pitch-black inside the sewer, the quality of the ghostly, monochrome vision the visor provided was remarkable. Nevertheless, Hoax was finding it hard to make out what the obstacle was.

'Let's shed a little light on the subject,' said Oddball. He tapped the cuff of his left gauntlet and it dispensed a tiny yellow capsule into his palm. A glo-cap. Oddball crushed it in his armoured glove to mix the chemicals in it together, then tossed it into the gloom ahead. The tunnel was suddenly brightly lit with a yellow glow, given off by the capsule as a result of the chemical reaction.

Hoax's visor immediately adjusted to the flood of bright light, to prevent him being dazzled. He could see that what lay ahead wasn't a cave-in, like the other blockages they had so far had to deal with. It was a grille of vertical metal bars, stretching right across the tunnel and from floor to ceiling.

The two boys waded forward to examine the grille more closely. Oddball gave it a firm tug. It was as solid as it looked. Judging by the metal's still-shiny finish, it had been installed only recently.

'But why would anyone go to the trouble of

blocking off a disused sewer?' puzzled Hoax.

Oddball shrugged.

'Dunno. But that glo-cap won't last long,' he said. 'And I've only got a few left. We'd better get cracking.'

He reached over his shoulder to release his warhammer from its clasps.

'I don't think even your hammer will shift that,' said Hoax, eyeing the grille doubtfully. 'It's heavy-duty stuff.'

'I'm not planning on bashing my way through,' replied Oddball.

With a series of twists and snaps, he separated his weapon into several sections. He passed all but one to Hoax to hold.

The final component – a cylindrical pin that secured the warhammer's head – rapidly transformed in Oddball's expert grasp into a tool like a sealant gun. He quickly ran its nozzle all the way round one of the grille's bars, applying a bead of red gel. He clicked the tool's flat end, then repeated the process. This time, blue gel oozed from the nozzle. As they came into contact, the gels began to fizz fiercely. Within seconds, their reaction had burned right through the metal bar.

Hoax watched impatiently as Oddball began tackling the other end of the bar. He only hoped they could still reach Griffin in time. Obstacles were not all that had hampered their progress through the tunnels. Twice, they had got lost. The map that Salt had given them – as a holographic overlay for Hoax's helmet visor – showed the original layout of the old City sewers. But in many places, the ancient tunnels had now collapsed. Elsewhere, service tunnels had been added. Within the first hour, they had found themselves at a junction that Hoax couldn't confidently match to his map.

'We can't know where to go next till we're sure exactly where we are now,' he had grumbled. 'I think you should use your wrist-stat, Oddball.'

The wrist-stat was one of Oddball's many ingenious inventions. It had a wide range of functions. One was the ability to obtain a satellite-based location fix. But doing so meant releasing a brief pulse of electrical energy from the device's tiny emergency battery.

Oddball had been reluctant.

'Salt said no electrics. We'd light up on the SeeBlock scanners for sure.'

'Only for a split second. Anything's better than

wandering around down here till we drop dead.'

In the end, Oddball had agreed. Hopefully, if anyone noticed the brief pulse of energy underground, they would think it was a mistake.

Less than an hour later they had found themselves at another mystery junction and had reached the same decision. Since then, they had been making good progress – until coming up against this annoying grille.

But Oddball was going great guns. He had already removed several lengths of bar. He yanked yet another section free and tossed it into the sludgy water. Hoax looked at the opening in the grille and gave a thumbs-up sign.

'Reckon that'll do it,' he said. 'Bit of a squeeze, perhaps . . .'

He led the way, easing himself carefully through the opening. Once through, he began wading forward along the murky tunnel again. The light from the glo-cap was dimming, as the fluorescent chemical reaction within it began to slow.

Oddball was a fair bit bigger than Hoax. He was still struggling through the grille when his friend gave a delighted cry.

'It dries out up here! The floor slopes upwards

until you're clear of the gloop. Boy, am I glad to— *WAAAH!'*

Oddball squeezed past the bars and hurriedly sloshed his way up the incline. Hoax was sprawled face-down on the tunnel floor.

'What happened?'

Hoax rolled over and sat up. He pointed to a black object lying on the tunnel floor.

'I fell over that, I guess!'

The black thing was only small – a fragment of something, by the looks of it. It didn't appear substantial enough to have tripped Hoax. Oddball stooped to take a closer look. He attempted to lift it. But despite its modest size, it was too heavy to move.

'Whatever it is, it's incredibly dense.' He snapped his visor's high-mag lenses into place and examined the material's surface. 'And it's organic, by the looks of it. Some sort of ultra-tough cellular tissue.'

'There's more over there,' said Hoax. He got to his feet and approached a much larger piece of the black substance further along the tunnel. 'This bit looks like part of some sort of shell. Must be the remains of something that died down here.

Judging by this, it must've been pretty huge.'

Oddball looked thoughtful.

'Do you remember that news story, a few months back, about something living in the Old City sewers?'

'Uh-huh,' affirmed Hoax. 'Our beloved Chairman sent down an extermination squad to sort it out. I remember him being very pleased with himself, as usual. Some rubbish about it "demonstrating the Perfect Corporation's tough stance on pest control". Why? D'you reckon this stuff is what's left of whatever it was?'

'Maybe. But there was a rumour at the time – I heard it from Shiv in the kitchens – that things didn't go nearly as smoothly as the Corporation made out. According to Shiv, not one of the White Knights that went into the tunnels came out again. He said the creature exterminated *them*, not the other way around.'

He looked from one fragment of black casing to the other.

'These *could* be the remains of an animal. But like you said, they look a lot like a body shell. An exo-skeleton, shed by something as it grew.'

Hoax was looking at his friend anxiously.

'What are you driving at?'

'What if the rumours were true?' replied Oddball. 'What if the Corporation didn't manage to kill whatever was down here. What if to hush up their botched operation, they just settled for isolating the thing in a particular tunnel section. Trapped it in. Behind bars . . .'

The glo-cap chose that moment to finally fail. The two boys were plunged into pitch darkness once more.

As his visor's night-sight kicked in again, Hoax anxiously scanned their surroundings. He heard Oddball suck in a long, deep breath through the hyper-sensitive nasal vents in his helmet.

'I'm picking up a strong organic scent. Something live, approaching fast.'

Despite Oddball's warning, the creature's attack caught Hoax unprepared. A monstrous black head suddenly burst from the gloom and took a ferocious snap at him with its pair of huge, serrated mandibles.

Hoax just managed to avoid being sliced in two by diving to his right. He rolled over – once, twice – then sprang back onto his feet. In an instant he had his slim fighting staff in a firm double-handed grip, ready to fend off the next attack.

'Oddball! Hit the lights!'

Oddball frantically emptied his glo-cap dispenser into his palm, clenched his fist around the half-dozen capsules to activate them and scattered them across the tunnel.

The sudden glare of the glo-caps' light was enough to cause the creature to recoil, dazzled. It also enabled the young Armouron to see their attacker clearly for the first time.

It wasn't a pretty sight.

The creature was all black and the size of a small vehicle. Its arching back was shielded by a thick shell of the tough material Hoax had stumbled across. It had no visible limbs – just an eyeless head, with its pair of huge, pincer-like mouthparts that had narrowly missed chopping Hoax in half.

Before the creature could recover, Hoax quickly took a fierce jab at it with his staff. But not quickly enough. The monster's left mandible batted the staff aside, knocking it from Hoax's grasp. The grotesque head darted forward again and Hoax found his upper body locked in the grip of its powerful jaws.

Only his armour saved him. In crafting Hoax's orange and black suit, Salt had focused on the cadet's talent for trickery. Hoax was one slippery customer – in his Armouron role as False-Light, his suit made him even more so. Its plastallic plates could shed their surface layer. By triggering this feature now, Hoax was able to wriggle free of the creature's grasp. The monster gave a screech of anger, spitting out thin slivers of armour.

Then it came at him again.

Oddball had now had time to gather up the pieces of his warhammer – Hoax had dropped them when he tripped. Within seconds, he had reassembled them. In a desperate attempt to save Hoax, he charged at the creature, yelling the knights' battle cry.

'*ARMOURON!*'

His mighty hammer crashed down on the beast's shelled back. But the only effect of Oddball's attack was to send a bone-cracking jolt through his own body. And to draw the creature's attention. It wheeled round to face him. Hoax seized the chance to grab his staff again and hurried to his friend's side.

'I don't think . . . we can . . . take it down,' panted Hoax. 'Its shell's too tough!'

The creature was now hanging back, making an odd *klee-klee-klee* noise, waiting for the best moment to strike. It was also blocking their route back to the grille.

'We'll have to run for it,' agreed Oddball. 'Further along the tunnel. Have you got anything to slow that thing down?'

Holding his staff with one hand, and without

taking his eyes off the creature, Hoax clicked open a suit flap under his right arm. He took out a handful of small foil-wrapped cubes.

'You betcha,' he said. 'OK. On the count of three, run like crazy. Ready? One . . . two . . . three . . . GO!'

Hoax flung the contents of his hand down in front of the sewer creature. It reared backwards as each cube exploded with a series of deafening bangs and crackling white flashes. The two boys turned on their heels and ran for their lives, into the pitch-black tunnel ahead.

Chapter 9
Going Solo

Salt had been right to worry. Tea-Leaf had indeed left the Academy. After slipping away from the mission briefing, she had made her way quickly through the Old School to the secret tunnel by which she always entered the complex. It led to the Academy garage, where she was now skulking in the shadow of one of the docked shuttlecraft.

She was already beginning to regret storming off. It served no real purpose. But the anger and frustration that Rake's continued criticism had stirred up had been overwhelming. She had just had to get away.

What's his problem? thought Tea-Leaf bitterly. *Why can't he accept me as one of the team?*

She wondered what Salt would make of her going off in a huff. He wasn't likely to be impressed. After a childhood of fending for herself on Nu-Topia's streets, the chance that the old armourer had offered Tea-Leaf to be part of the Armouron team, to *belong* somewhere, meant more to her than she liked to admit. And now, thanks to Rake, she might have spoiled everything.

If only he'd give me a break. The others don't treat me like I'm an idiot.

She tried to pull herself together. The damage was done. She needed to get her head straight and move on. She must find a way to win back Salt's good opinion and gain Rake's respect.

Maybe if I could pull off something really challenging . . . something that helps the mission . . . That would prove to them that I'm worth having around.

A daring scheme was beginning to take shape in her mind.

If Rake thought she wasn't ready to be part of this mission, she would show him how wrong he was.

With a new sense of purpose, Tea-Leaf made her way swiftly and silently to the garage exit. She slipped out into the street and hurried along it towards the stadium's main public entrance.

On a fight day, like yesterday, the area outside the entrance was a noisy chaos of jostling Gladiator fans. Today, it was deserted. The taxi rank on the opposite side of the street was quiet. Only three of its twenty drop-docks were occupied.

Of the three vehicles that stood silently charging their power cells, two were standard cabs, designed to carry up to four passengers. The third was a single-seater – a tiny egg-shaped pod.

Tea-Leaf slunk across to the smaller vehicle and hit its door release. The clear canopy that formed the cab's upper half slid back. She quickly slipped into its snug interior. The canopy closed smoothly and an eager, artificial voice filled the cab.

'Hello there! I'm FabCab 482 and I'll be your ride today! And remember – with PerfectCorp transport systems, every ride is a perfect ride!'

Tea-Leaf had already taken a small pair of wire-cutters from a compartment in her suit's breastplate. She used them to prise open a panel in the cab's left side. It had been a while since Nip – a fellow street-child – had first shown her how to hotwire a cab. She had done it twice since, but not recently. But as the panel came free, to reveal the circuitry within, she felt a flood of relief. *Layout looks more or less the same – shouldn't be too difficult to find the right wires . . .*

She had no intention of *stealing* the cab, she told herself. She was just borrowing it. For a worthy cause.

As she studied the muddle of electronics, the cab's chirpy voice prattled on.

'For your safety, all FabCab journeys must be authorized by Transport Control . . .'

Tea-Leaf located the lead she was after.

'. . . Please state your destination, followed by your Citizen PIN.'

The aim was to cut the power to the cab's main processor. This would immediately register back at the city's Transport Control Centre as a unit failure – a breakdown. The cab would be logged as out of order and a technician would be sent out to fix it.

In the meantime, if she could reconnect the power to the motor systems only, she should be able to gain manual control. With luck, she could have the cab underway, with its tracking signal disabled, long before 'assistance' arrived.

She gingerly moved her snippers over the thin

red power cable. They slipped from her nervous grasp.

'Stupid clacking things!'

She scrabbled frantically about for them.

'I'm sorry, I didn't quite get that! Did you say two hundred and thir—'

The voice cut off and the soft purr of the cab's systems died. Tea-Leaf had salvaged the snippers and cut the cable. First stage completed.

Two minutes more and the rewiring was finished. As Tea-Leaf reconnected the power, the thrum of the tiny pod's maglev motors kicked in again. But no more irritating voice.

Tea-Leaf yanked open part of the cab's interior trim to reveal a small red-knobbed joystick. This was the manual control. It was usually only used by garage technicians to move the vehicle around when its systems were offline, during manufacture or repair.

Tea-Leaf clutched the joystick and tweaked it up and to the right. The cab disengaged from its drop-dock, rose half a metre above the ground and swung out into the street. She had control.

Almost an hour later, Tea-Leaf was crouching in

the shadow of the looming rear wall of the West One Peace Keep. She had ditched the FabCab a few miles back. Her journey through the city's west quarter had passed without mishap. But driving right up to the doorstep of a Corporation fortress wouldn't have been very smart. She had covered the last two miles on foot, making full use of her suit's amazing properties of camouflage and stealth.

Now that she was up close to the Keep, her great idea didn't seem so great. Her aim was to get inside somehow, hack into the main computer control systems and find a way to override the containment field. Salt's plan to sabotage the field generator was sound, but infiltrating the very heart of Decimal's control centre was more direct – and more bold. Surely Salt and Rake would *have* to be impressed if she took out the field single-handedly.

But first she had to get in.

There was no entrance at ground level in this face of the Keep. But about ten metres above Tea-Leaf's head, a small docking platform jutted out from the building's sheer black wall. A narrow corridor led from it into the Keep.

Tea-Leaf peeled back the sleeves of thin film that covered each of her gauntlets' fingertips. This exposed the high-grip pads beneath. She reached high with her right hand and pressed it against the wall. As she let her arm take her weight, the micro-pores in the fingertip pads held fast to the smooth surface.

She pulled herself up until her right shoulder was level with her gripping hand, then stretched even higher with the other. Again, it gripped powerfully. As she transferred her weight to this arm and relaxed the other, her right gauntlet's fingertips released their hold.

Hand over hand, half a metre at a time, Tea-Leaf hauled herself up the sheer, glassy wall. She reached the platform and peered cautiously over its edge.

There was nobody in sight. Tea-Leaf was about to haul herself onto the platform when she felt a sudden rush of energy pulse through her chest. It was the Flow, coming from her medallion. It was warning her of something.

She took another peek over the balcony's edge. This time she spotted it. A small silver dome was mounted in the ceiling of the corridor. It housed a set of tiny surveillance cameras. They were tirelessly scanning the corridor's entrance.

Tea-Leaf clung to the platform with one hand. With the other, she swung her crossbow around from her back to her front. She snapped open one of its ammunition chambers and plucked something from inside. It was a tiny ball of sticky green gel, with an even tinier black dot at its very centre.

Tea-Leaf primed the bow then loaded the gel ball in place of its usual bolt. She raised the weapon awkwardly, with one hand, over the platform edge. She took aim and fired.

The missile hit the silver camera dome and stuck fast. Success. While the ball clung in place, its tiny magnetized core – the dark dot – would create enough interference to turn the camera's output signal into meaningless fuzz. But the gel coating was designed to stick only temporarily. The pull of gravity would cause it to slowly peel away. When it finally released its grip, the ball would fall to the floor – at which point normal camera service would resume.

Security would hopefully dismiss the brief signal failure as a technical hiccup. Even if they did investigate, the tiny gel ball was likely to remain unnoticed, or even be squished underfoot, leaving no evidence of foul play.

Already, the sticky goo was beginning to peel away. Tea-Leaf had about a minute to get clear.

She swung herself up onto the platform and hurried into the corridor. There were bound to be more security cameras further along. She needed to get out of their field of view somehow – and quickly.

Looking up, she found what she was looking for. A cover panel in the ceiling. Using her high-grip gauntlets once more, she quickly scaled the corridor's smooth wall and rattled the ceiling panel loose.

She pulled herself up and across into the cavity above the panel, then slid it back into place – only a split second before her goo-ball hit the floor.

Curled in the cramped, dark ceiling cavity, Tea-Leaf let out a long breath. She slipped her visor's night-vision overlay into place – and felt an immediate rush of excitement. Things were working out better than she could have hoped. The cavity carried bundle upon bundle of computer cables. There was a good chance that one of them would let her connect to the Keep's main network. She might be able to finish the job from here . . .

Tea-Leaf hurriedly slipped her roll-up keyboard from her suit's leg compartment. She pulled out its magnetic hack-patch, wrapped it around the nearest cable bundle and set to work.

Chapter 10
A Rough Ride

'Ow! Your sword hilt is sticking in my side!'

'Sorry,' whispered Rake. He shifted his body awkwardly in an attempt to give Snow a bit more room. But it was impossible to find any extra space – the inside of the shuttle's undercarriage housing was painfully cramped. It was pitch-black too. There were definitely more pleasant ways to travel.

It had been Salt's idea that they stow away like this. He had discovered that a news crew from PerfectVision – the Corporation's official media group – was being sent out to report on the Epsilon 'catastrophe'. Their shuttle was being readied for departure from PerfectVision's city headquarters.

There was just enough time for Rake and Snow to sneak the few blocks from the Academy to the media building and secretly hitch a lift.

They had climbed the shuttle's right rear landing-foot and hidden in its housing. When the landing gear had been raised after take-off, it had proved quite a squash.

Even so, Rake had to admit there was no other way they could have reached their target destination – the containment field generator – so quickly.

Snow let out another groan as their hiding place juddered violently yet again. 'This is the last time I fly PerfectVision!' she hissed. 'Do you think we're nearly there?'

'Must be by now. In fact, it feels like we're coming down, doesn't it?'

Sure enough, there was a sudden pneumatic hiss. Light flooded the compartment as the undercarriage doors below them split apart.

Rake and Snow flattened themselves against the shuttle's internal frame and clung on. With the whir of powerful servos, the hefty landing-foot beside them slowly swung down and locked in position.

Through the open hatch, the children could see the ground approaching fast. There was a roar of engine noise and a rush of warm updraught as the landing thrusters kicked in.

'As soon as we touch, get clear!' yelled Rake over the din. Snow nodded.

The giant metal foot *whumped* down, absorbing the impact as the shuttle settled on the dusty ground. Rake and Snow dropped silently from their hiding place. They landed lightly and scurried away beneath the craft's belly, towards its rear.

The shuttle had put down not far from a cluster of fuel dumps. A quick dash brought the two cadets to the nearest. They ducked behind a stack of fuel cells. From the safety of their hiding place, they scanned their surroundings.

Less than half a kilometre to the west, the Peace Keep rose up from the lifeless landscape. The area around it was a hive of military activity. Rake could make out as many as twenty White Knight troop carriers. In the far distance, beyond the fortress, they could see an arching wall of luminous green light. It rose skyward, curving back and to both sides to form a vast dome of fizzing energy.

An opening appeared in the side of the PerfectVision shuttle. A ramp extended smoothly from it. Rake and Snow watched as the team of reporters and technicians headed down it, lugging their equipment.

'The Chairman will have hand-picked his own tame journalists, of course,' said Snow. 'And PerfectVision will no doubt be the only media organization allowed anywhere near. That way the Corporation will have complete control over any broadcast.'

'Uh-huh,' agreed Rake. 'With the right camera shots, and some clever editing, they'll be able to put together whatever angle the Chairman tells them to. He'll make sure the public sees something that backs up his phoney disaster story.'

A hover barge carrying three White Knights came skimming up to the shuttle crew. After a brief exchange of words, the PerfectVision crew boarded the vehicle. It zoomed away towards the base of the energy dome.

'Never mind – they're not our problem,' continued Rake. He turned to look due north. About a hundred metres away, a squat grey cubic structure the size of a large building sat on a colossal crawler platform. Its upper surface was covered with groups of white dish antennae, like clumps of strange mushrooms.

Rake dropped his helmet's zoom visor into place and slowly scanned the peculiar construction.

'That's the field generator all right,' he said. 'And I think I can see our way in – a ventilation outlet about two-thirds of the way up its near side. Our only problem is him . . .'

Even with unassisted vision, Snow could see the man – a human, not a White Knight. He was standing with his back to them in front of the generator's massive, caterpillar-tracked base.

'Looks like he's servicing the crawler platform,' reported Rake. 'There's no chance of us getting in unnoticed with him there. Any ideas?'

He turned to consult Snow – and found her with one hand laid across her breastplate, covering her medallion. Her eyes had a slightly glazed look. A moment later her expression cleared and she let her hand drop.

'Don't worry,' she said. 'He's nearly done. He's about to move on to the opposite face.'

Rake gave her a bemused look, then looked

back at the technician. Through his zoom lenses, he watched the man replace a laser-spanner in his tool belt, then move off, heading around the front of the crawler towards its other side.

Rake turned back to Snow, frowning. 'How did you . . . ?'

'I'm not sure,' said Snow, a little self-consciously. 'I just had a feeling that was what he was thinking. Come on!'

And without saying any more, she sprinted away towards the field generator, keeping low.

Rake set off after her, still unsure quite what had just happened.

Chapter 11
A Pinch of Salt

Salt hated dealing with androids. This one, in particular, was about as helpful as a poke in the eye.

'The Director is unavailable at the present time,' it said, smiling sweetly. It was an administration model, programmed to deal calmly and efficiently with all enquiries – to an extent that was totally infuriating.

'This is important,' growled Salt. He dumped the shoulder guards he had spent the last two hours repairing onto the desk in front of the robotic administrator with a clatter. 'Lanista specifically instructed me to deliver these spaulders to her, in person, the moment they were ready.'

'Regrettably, she is not on the premises,' replied the android cheerily.

Salt could really do without this. He had hoped to return Lanista's armour as quickly as possible. It was vital that he continue his search for Tea-Leaf. By now, the others would be well into the mission.

It struck Salt as rather odd that Lanista was not here at Corporation HQ. She had clearly told him to bring her repaired armour to her here. What had drawn her away unexpectedly?

The old Armouron warrior felt an intuitive sense of dread. Had she somehow rumbled their secret rescue operation?

He tried again.

'If she's not here, can you tell me where she is, please? I'll take them to her there.'

The administrator's fixed smile didn't waver.

'The Director has not requested that she have her location disclosed.'

Salt decided to try another angle. 'Fine. But I wouldn't want to be in your boots when she finds out I tried to follow her orders and you got in my way.'

The android didn't respond immediately. It

wasn't used to threats. Salt guessed it was running a full analysis of the situation.

He knew that as a machine, the robot had no sense of self-preservation or fear. It would, however, be programmed to avoid getting damaged. The Corporation liked to keep repair costs down. And if it had served at HQ for any length of time, it would know that annoying the Chairman's hot-tempered sister was a sure way to get damaged.

As he had hoped, the administrator abruptly changed its tune. It had clearly found no specific instruction to keep Lanista's whereabouts secret.

'The Director is leading Peace Squad T-16 in an investigation into unauthorized activity in the disused sewer system,' it informed Salt, still beaming. 'I calculate that her probable destination is the West One Peace Keep.'

Salt felt a swell of anxiety. She was in the Old City sewers. She must have picked up Hoax and Oddball's trail somehow.

This changed everything. His search for Tea-Leaf would have to wait.

'Right. Thank you.' He tried to remain outwardly calm. 'In that case, I'll need to get this armour to her there. I'll need my travel authorizing. Can you do that from here?'

'Since you are fulfilling a request from a member of the Board, that should not present a problem. What is the registration of the vehicle you will be using?'

'I'll take the *Sieger*. Plate AC5079.'

The android pulled a slim fibre-optic cable from its waist and plugged it into a port in the desk. A few seconds passed. Then it disconnected and addressed Salt once again.

'I have successfully obtained clearance for that journey for you: shuttlecraft AC5079 from its current location – the Academy, Central Five – to the West One Peace Keep. Your return trip has also been authorized.'

'Thanks,' growled Salt. He swept up the spaulders from the desk in his bear-like arms and turned to leave.

'Have a nice day!' chirruped the administrator.

Salt gave a gruff snort. That was looking less likely by the second.

Chapter 12
Skirterville

Hoax heaved aside the rusted cover above him then climbed two more ladder rungs to poke his head out of the airshaft. Blinking back the sunlight, he gratefully filled his lungs with fresh air. He had never been so pleased to see the sky – even if it was an unnatural one, masked by the green haze of the containment field.

'Get a move on,' said Oddball, prodding him from below. 'If I spend any more time down here, I'm going to lose it.'

Hoax clambered out of the musty shaft, closely followed by his friend.

'I thought we were stuck down there for ever!' said Oddball. He stretched his long limbs gratefully.

The encounter with the sewer creature had badly shaken both boys. Their desperate flight along the tunnel following its attack had brought them to a second barred grille. It had taken Oddball several nerve-jangling minutes to cut through it. Hoax had spent every second expecting the monster to rear up out of the blackness and finish them off.

But their firework display had evidently left the creature more wary than they realized. They had made it past the grille without it putting in another appearance.

'And it's still trapped in that section,' Oddball had insisted, as much to reassure himself as Hoax. 'It's way too big to get through the holes I cut.'

Nevertheless, they had pressed on through the tunnels with renewed haste. The glo-caps were all gone now, so they had been forced to rely on visor-vision to find the way. Their spirits had sunk on finding their planned route back to the surface blocked by yet another cave-in – until they discovered this alternative airshaft, run-down but passable.

Out in the open, Oddball checked his wrist-stat.

'It's taken us way longer than we hoped to get through. We've only got just over an hour till the others shut down the field zone.'

He scanned their surroundings. They had come up near the centre of the area enclosed by the energy field. Oddball could see the crumbling remains of the Epsilon power station just a few hundred metres to the north.

He slid open a panel in his suit and drew out the clockwork beetle.

'I'll check its departure coordinates again, so we can track down Griffin's lot.'

Hoax was looking past his friend, a little anxiously. 'Erm . . . I don't think that's going to be a problem . . .'

Oddball turned. Several rather wild-looking men and women had appeared from nowhere. They were closing in on the boys in a semi-circle. All were weather-beaten and dressed in scruffy, worn-out clothes. But they had the look of people whose hardship had only made them tougher. Most were armed with weapons made from cleverly adapted pieces of junk.

The exception was the man leading their advance. He was tall and striking, with broad shoulders and dark skin and hair. The left cheek of his stubbled face was marked with a long pale scar. And he was brandishing a genuine weapon – a heavy, two-handed Gladiatorial sword.

Hoax looked at the several makeshift bows aimed in his direction.

'Whoa! Don't shoot!' He hastily raised both hands in the air. 'We're friends!'

The scar-faced man looked them up and down, clearly aware of the armour they were wearing. He eyed them suspiciously and didn't lower his weapon.

'We've got a message for you,' Hoax pressed on, 'from Salt!'

'You're friends of Salt?' The man's voice was deep and rich.

'Are you kidding?' Hoax grinned nervously. 'He's like family, the big ol' softy!'

The man looked less than convinced by Hoax's description.

'Prove it.'

Oddball quickly held up the clockwork beetle.

'How about this? It sought out Salt last night. From the message it carried, we figured it came from an old friend of his. Someone in trouble who needed a helping hand.'

The man looked at the beetle. A moment later, his stern expression dissolved into a warm smile. He sheathed his sword.

'You were right on both counts.' He bowed his head formally. 'I'm Griffin. Welcome to Skirterville.'

Hoax returned his nod, but gave no name.

Oddball was still clutching the beetle. 'I've gotta ask,' he blurted. 'Which one of you made this? It's an absolute masterpiece!'

Hoax looked apologetically at Griffin.

'Sorry. He's a bit of a techno-geek.'

Griffin smiled, then answered Oddball.

'The beetle was built by one of my comrades. A man called Tock – *our* techno-geek. He crafted it some years ago. It has carried many messages in its time, but none so urgent as the one I sent Salt yesterday.'

His expression became grave.

'Unfortunately, Tock was badly injured during the beetle's dispatch. To make sure it penetrated the containment field, he had to get up close. He was trying to make his way back when a White Knight picked him off. We got him back to base camp, but he hasn't regained consciousness.'

'I'm sorry to hear that,' said Oddball. 'Judging by this, he's a genius.'

Griffin nodded. 'And a good friend. He's also the only one of our group with enough technical know-how to get the *Inimitable* off the ground. Without Tock, I fear our escape plans are futile.'

'The *Inimitable*?' queried Hoax.

'Our ship,' explained Griffin. 'The "wings" I mentioned in my message. We've been building her over the last few weeks – ever since we suspected that the Corporation had located our base. We knew they'd come after us and that we needed to get clear before they did. But we hadn't bargained on this blasted containment field . . .'

'Don't give up just yet,' said Oddball. 'If things are going to plan, our friends are making a few adjustments to Decimal's precious field right now. With a bit of luck, you should have your escape "door" in precisely . . .'

He consulted his wrist-stat once more.

'. . . seventy-three minutes. So you'd best get me to this ship of yours. I can't promise that I'm a match for your friend Tock, but I'm fairly handy with a toolkit. Show me where she is and I'll get her in the air somehow.'

Griffin looked a little doubtful.

'He's not kidding,' Hoax assured him. 'If it's a machine, he'll get it working. Like I said, he's a *real* techno-geek . . .'

Griffin hesitated, then nodded.

'All right. If Salt sent you to help, I must trust his judgement. And I believe I recognize his handiwork in the armour you wear . . . Follow me.'

And he turned and strode away towards the derelict buildings.

Fifteen minutes later, the boys were back underground. The Skirters had first led them to the ground-level ruins of the old reactor hall, which had once housed the Epsilon power station's main control centre. There wasn't much of it left. The roof was entirely missing. But an elevator in one corner of the hall had recently been restored to working order. It had carried Griffin and the cadets down into a large chamber below, where the reactor itself had once stood. Right now, the chamber held something altogether different – a giant, ramshackle airship.

Oddball let out a low whistle.

'I can see why you call her the *Inimitable*,' he said. 'I've certainly never come across anything quite like her before!'

Griffin gave a wry smile.

'She's a bit . . . *unusual*, I'll admit. Built entirely from parts scavenged from the Dumps. Tock put her together around an old FF1 Flying Fortress hull we dug up – a wreck from the Wars, I think.'

'How did you ever get her in here?' marvelled Hoax.

'A piece at a time,' answered Griffin. 'Tock's team stripped down the hull, then assembled her here, component by component.'

'More to the point,' said Oddball, 'how do you plan to get her out? Assuming we can get her off the ground, that is.'

Griffin gestured to the chamber's heavy ceiling.

'The roof was originally designed to slide

back – so that the reactor could be lifted out for upgrading. Tock managed to repair the mechanism so the roof doors work again – with a bit of coaxing.'

'OK,' said Oddball purposefully. 'I guess I better see what I can do with her.'

He checked his wrist-stat again. 'We really haven't got long now. Mister Griffin, sir, can you round up your people and get them on board? I'll try to get her air-worthy before our time runs out . . .'

With that, he clambered up onto one of the *Inimitable*'s stubby wings, yanked off an engine hood and began examining the mechanism within.

Hoax hurried back to the elevator with Griffin. Up in the hall above, they set about gathering together the fifty or so Skirters. Griffin instructed them to collect their belongings and go down to the reactor chamber to board the ship. Several were injured and had to be carried on board.

As they were checking the area for the final time, to be sure they hadn't missed anyone, Hoax asked Griffin why the Corporation was so keen to get rid of him.

'My comrades and I stand for the things the Corporation hates,' replied the exiled Gladiator. 'Freedom of thought and speech; justice; equality. Just like you and your fellow Armouron.'

Griffin smiled at Hoax's look of surprise.

'Yes, my young friend – I recognize the emblem on your breastplate. You serve a long and noble tradition. Salt has done well to revive your order. Earth needs the Armouron now more than ever.'

He returned to Hoax's question.

'It's not just that, though. The Chairman and his sister have their own reasons for wanting me dead. Lanista never forgave me for defeating her in the Arena. And for a long time I have done my best to cause her brother as much embarrassment as I can.' He gave another smile. 'I suspect that this campaign is personal.'

'Oh, it's personal all right, you lowlife!' shrieked a menacing voice.

Hoax and Griffin spun round.

On the far side of the hall, flanked by four filth-spattered White Knights, stood the bedraggled, wild-eyed figure of Lanista.

Chapter 13
Fighting Time

'Garrgghh!'

Rake let out a snarl of frustration. He gave the thick bundle of cables that spewed from the ducting an angry slap.

'Anything I can do?' asked Snow from below.

Rake swung his legs over the ducting and dropped to the floor beside her.

'It's driving me nuts! I'm ninety-nine per cent certain I've found the wiring for the right shield zone,' he said. 'The one that Hoax and Oddball are expecting us to shut down. But I can't figure out a way to do it temporarily.'

He checked the dial of the tiny, super-accurate clockwork timer in his suit's forearm guard.

'And we're running out of time – fast!'

He looked back up at the cables dangling above him. He traced their ducting back to where it joined a large barrel-shaped power cell on the far side of the room.

'Maybe we should just take the direct approach and knock out the main cells permanently.'

'Master Salt insisted that we shouldn't leave traces,' said Snow. 'I guess that was why he'd put Tea-Leaf in our team. She's the one with the real knack for this sort of thing – hacking systems invisibly.'

'Yeah, I know,' said Rake, a little irritably. He didn't need reminding that his quarrel with Tea-Leaf now looked like jeopardizing the success of the mission.

'What if we tried to short-circuit the—'

'LOOK OUT!'

Snow gave Rake a sudden two-handed shove in the chest. As he staggered back, a bolt of red energy fizzed narrowly past him.

A pair of White Knights were patrolling the field generator's unmanned areas. They had stumbled on the young Armouron. As the first android prepared to fire another shot, the other reached for its throat, to activate its comlink and report to control.

Rake and Snow moved like lightning. Rake's shortsword was out of its scabbard and slicing down onto the first android's blaster arm in the blink of an eye. Arm and blaster tumbled to the floor.

Snow whipped out her T-shaped tonfa fighting stick. She delivered a ferocious jab to the other Knight's neck, crushing its communicator. A second fierce blow left a deep split in the android's armoured visor.

But the robots were fast too. The one fighting Rake managed to grab the cadet's sword arm with its remaining hand. It gave it a violent twist. Now it was Rake's weapon that clattered to the floor.

Snow's opponent smashed a metal fist into her breastplate, sending her sprawling across the floor. She struggled back into a sitting position in time to see the White Knight draw its blaster and take aim at Rake, who was still grappling with the other android.

In a desperate bid to save her friend, Snow aimed her tonfa and pressed its release catch. A length of rope shot out from the stick's end.

It wrapped itself round the White Knight's blaster arm. Snow gave the rope a sharp tug. The android's arm jerked to the side, sending its shot off target. The red energy bolt struck its partner. The robot slumped forward – trapping Rake beneath its lifeless body.

The second android raised its left hand. A thin blade flicked out from its edge. The White Knight sliced through Snow's rope, then strode to where she was hurriedly getting back to her feet. It lashed out at her tonfa arm with a fierce kick. There was a sickening crack. Snow screamed – and fell back on the ground.

The White Knight turned its attention back to Rake. He was still struggling to get out from under the heavy robotic body pinning him down. There was nothing he could do as the second android strode to stand over him and took careful aim at his head with its blaster.

There was a *fssssh-thunk* and a ten-centimetre-long metal bolt suddenly appeared in the split in the White Knight's visor. The android went down like a sack of potatoes, with sparks crackling from its head.

Rake craned his neck to see where the life-saving shot had come from.

Tea-Leaf was standing in the doorway. She was holding her crossbow.

She hurried to where Rake lay, crouched down and helped roll the slumped Knight off him.

'You OK?'

'Yeah, I think so,' said Rake. He sat up slowly. 'Thanks.'

There was a low moan from the other side of the

room. Snow was sitting up, nursing her right arm. Her face was pale and clammy. Tea-Leaf and Rake hurried to check on her.

'I think that kick dislocated my elbow,' she murmured. 'My armour contracted around it and it popped back.' She gave a brave smile. 'It's not too bad now. If I set my suit to keep it immobilized, I'll be OK.'

The others helped her to her feet. Rake looked at the two wrecked androids and the damage caused by their brief fight. He gave an ironic chuckle.

'So much for us not leaving any evidence behind!'

'Kettle patrols check in with control at regular intervals,' said Tea-Leaf. 'We've got maybe ten minutes before they send backup, if we're lucky.'

Rake checked his timer again.

'And even less than that before Oddball and Hoax are expecting the field to be deactivated.'

He suddenly became all action.

'Let's face it, we've blown the softly-softly approach. There's no reason now why we shouldn't just cut the main power feeds and take out the whole field.'

He reached for his sword. But Tea-Leaf grabbed his arm.

'No!' she urged. 'You mustn't! It's booby-trapped! If you cut the power, the field will implode – the entire dome will collapse inward. There's enough energy in it to frazzle everything and everyone inside it!'

'How could you know that?' said Rake, puzzled.

Tea-Leaf looked sheepish. 'I hacked into the network in the West One Keep. I was trying to shut off the field zone from there. That's when I found out that the system is designed to be tamper-proof.'

Rake looked crestfallen. His shoulders slumped.

'We've failed, then.'

'I didn't say that,' said Tea-Leaf. There was a steely look in her eyes. 'I couldn't override the field generator controls from the Keep. But I'm pretty certain I can shut down the zone from here in the generator itself.'

Rake held her determined gaze for a moment. He gave a firm nod.

'OK. Do it. Snow and I will watch your back.'

He gave Tea-Leaf a leg-up onto the ducting above. As she hurriedly unfurled her roll-up keypad once more and wrapped its hack-patch around the cable bundle, Rake managed a nervous smile.

'You've got just over seven minutes, so no pressure . . .'

Chapter 14
Flight of the *Inimitable*

Lanista's expression as she advanced on Griffin was one of pure hatred.

'Do you have *any* idea what I've been through to track you down?' she spat.

Her wild-eyed glare was fixed on the Skirter leader as though he was a tiny rodent and she a ravenous hawk.

'I'll tell you, shall I? I've spent over an hour wading through the most revolting, foul-smelling muck I've ever had the misfortune to come upon! On top of that . . .' she raved, 'I've had a most unpleasant encounter with some sort of grotesque, overgrown cockroach!'

She raised her left arm high to display a long,

bloody gash in her side.

'But do you know what?' She came to a halt a few metres from her old enemy. A crazed smile spread across her pale face. '*It was worth it.*'

She reached over her left shoulder, grasped the hilt of her ion-sica and unsheathed its curving, red-edged blade.

'Because now I'm going to bring your miserable life to an overdue end!'

She took a step forward aggressively, then suddenly stopped. She seemed to have fully noticed Hoax for the first time. Her gaze moved across his orange and black armour to the medallion in his breastplate. A momentary look of surprise – even alarm – flickered in her fiery eyes.

'*Armouron!*' she hissed poisonously. 'My brother said your kind had crawled back out from under a stone somewhere! I see they are enlisting *infants* now!'

Hoax gave a defiant smile.

'Better young and keen than old and mean.'

Lanista glowered at him.

'My fight is with Griffin today. But I'll be only too happy to dispatch you too, if you get in my way!'

She began to advance again, brandishing her lethal weapon. But Griffin made no attempt to draw his own. He simply stood his ground.

'We settled our differences in the Arena, over ten years ago,' he said calmly. 'I have no wish to fight you again.'

'Oh, but you *will* fight me!' spat Lanista. She signalled to her team of White Knights. They immediately levelled their blasters at Hoax. 'Or your young friend here will pay the price!'

Griffin scowled. After a moment's pause, he reluctantly drew his double-handed sword from its scabbard.

'And *this* time,' Lanista hissed, 'I'll give you more than that pretty little scar I left you with!'

With a sudden blood-curdling screech she lunged at Griffin, slicing her ion-sica at his left side. The Skirter leader side-stepped expertly, parrying her blow. He quickly seized the initiative and swept his own heavy blade in a fierce uppercut. Only his opponent's impressive speed enabled her to dodge it.

The fight raged on, blade clashing against blade again and again. Hoax watched helplessly. Lanista had clearly set her vengeful heart on a rematch against her old foe. If he tried to intervene, her bodyguards would shoot him where he stood. For the moment, he had no choice but to watch.

Griffin was forced backwards as Lanista rained blows down on him. Her eyes flashed wildly with each strike. She broke off her attack at last, stepping back to sneer at her panting opponent.

'Not so cocky now, are you, Mister People's Champion?'

Griffin straightened up, breathing heavily. 'Your swordsmanship has improved since our last meeting, I confess,' he said. 'But you fight with anger, not honour – as you always did.'

Lanista seethed.

'Let's see how your precious *honour* copes with *this*!' she shrieked.

Hoax looked on in horror as she charged at Griffin once again, whirling her glowing sword like a berserker.

But as she bore down on him, Griffin suddenly came to life. He dodged Lanista's first swing and used his right leg to trip her. Her ion-sica slipped from her grasp as she stumbled. A moment later, she was flat on her back with Griffin's sword at her throat. Now it was his eyes that burned fiercely.

'I have no desire to kill you,' he growled. 'But I will do so. Unless you call off your guards and allow me and my comrades safe passage to leave.'

Lanista looked like she might explode with anger. But she wasn't in a position to argue. Staring lividly at her enemy, she gave a sharp nod.

'Do I have your word?' pressed Griffin.

'Yes!' spat the incensed woman. She flashed a look at her robot bodyguard. As one, they lowered their blasters.

Griffin moved his sword from Lanista's throat. She squirmed away, crawling back to join her android guards. As she got to her feet, she cast a look of utter loathing at Griffin. At that moment, Hoax realized that her word meant nothing.

'KILL THEM BOTH!'

Hoax only had the split second it took the White Knights to register Lanista's command to act. But it was enough.

One unique feature of his Armouron suit was its helmet's ability to manipulate sound. He could use it to throw his voice, or mimic the patterns of people's speech. Now he combined both these effects in a bid to distract his enemies.

He threw his voice to the area behind the White Knights, imitating the familiar tones of the Chairman.

'STOP! HOLD YOUR FIRE!'

The trick worked beautifully. Lanista and her bodyguards turned in surprise, convinced that the Corporation boss had just arrived on the scene. Their momentary distraction was all Hoax and Griffin needed.

With lightning speed, the young Armouron unclipped a canister from his suit belt and hurled it at the White Knights' feet. It burst open on impact, splattering an oily, colourless liquid across the floor.

The androids had now processed the fact that they'd been duped. They turned back to confront Hoax and Griffin. As they did so, their feet lost grip in the pool of anti-friction liquid. All four went sprawling. Their blasters clattered from their grasp as they hit the floor.

Hoax swiftly drew his fighting staff and advanced. A well-aimed jab to a weak spot below the first White Knight's jaw deactivated it before it could react. As the second android floundered on the slippery surface, Hoax shortened and snapped his staff, converting it into a nunchaku. He delivered a whiplash blow with the chain-linked sticks. The robot slumped to the floor and lay still.

Griffin too had been quick to act. His sword had already put the last two White Knights out of action.

But Hoax's heart sank, as together he and Griffin turned to confront Lanista – only to find that she had managed to grab one of the dropped blasters.

'Do I have to do *everything* myself?' she complained, raising the weapon. She curled her finger around its trigger.

Suddenly, the floor beneath them shuddered violently. Thrown off balance, Lanista shot wide. She cursed, took aim again, then tottered to one side as the floor once more moved under her feet. And this time, its motion continued. It was accompanied by the low rumble and protesting squeal of machinery.

'The launch doors!' yelled Griffin, struggling to keep his feet as the floor lurched. 'They're opening the doors!'

Sure enough, a widening crack was now visible along the centre of the hall's floor. The ceiling doors of the reactor chamber below were slowly but surely sliding apart. They sped up a little and the gap widened quickly. Lanista, stranded on its far side, was struggling desperately to keep her feet as the section of floor on which she was standing rolled back into the wall. The blaster fell from her hand and slid away from her.

The noise of the door mechanism was suddenly drowned out by a much louder roar. It was the roar of the *Inimitable*'s engines. Hoax and Griffin staggered to the edge of the moving floor, in time to see the bizarre craft lift off awkwardly from the reactor chamber below. She wobbled, like a nervous skater, then quickly rose.

From a hatch in the ship's side, which looked like it was made from an old fridge door, hung one of Griffin's men. As the *Inimitable* rose through the gap in the ceiling doors, he reached out his arm.

'Come on!' he yelled. 'Get in!'

With his help, first Hoax, then Griffin boarded the hovering craft. Hoax scrambled across to a glass casserole porthole in the ship's starboard side and looked out at the chaotic scene they were leaving behind.

One of the four White Knights had managed to reactivate. It was floundering pathetically in the pool of Lo-Fric liquid, even less able to get to its feet now the floor was moving beneath it. Behind the stricken androids, the remaining walls of the derelict building were beginning to shake and crumble, destabilized by the *Inimitable*'s thrusters.

Lanista was tottering on the brink of the sliding floor, watching their escape with a look of insane rage on her face.

Hoax watched with horror as the deranged woman took a step back, then launched herself in a desperate leap. Her long, thin arms were at full stretch, her fingers curled like claws to clutch at the ship's hull.

It was a jump that no ordinary human could make. Even Snow, fully suited, would have struggled to clear the distance. But fuelled by hatred, the Chairman's sister almost made it.

Lanista's bloodcurdling scream as she plummeted into the reactor chamber below was drowned out by a sudden rise in engine volume. The *Inimitable* thundered up and away, rising fast into the sky above the ruined plant.

Hoax and Griffin made their way forward towards the ship's cockpit with some difficulty. The ramshackle ship was shaking violently and every centimetre of her was crammed with Skirter bodies. When they finally made it to the cramped cabin, they found Oddball at the ship's

preposterous control console. He was perched on the pilot's seat – an old fuel canister – frantically pulling levers and flicking switches. He had removed his helmet and was sweating heavily.

'You did it!' Hoax yelled at his friend. 'You got her working!'

Oddball mopped his brow and grinned.

'Just about! Although I'd never have got her fired up without Tock here talking me through it! Thank clack he came round when he did.'

He gestured to a man lying on a makeshift stretcher against the cockpit wall. He looked in a bad way, but cheerful. Griffin crouched to greet him warmly.

'I'm setting a course for the field zone that Salt told the others to deactivate,' said Oddball. 'At this speed, it should only take us a couple of minutes to get there.'

He flicked a final switch then sat back, blowing out his cheeks.

'I just hope Rake and Snow fulfil their part of the bargain. Neither of them will find messing with a Corporation system as simple as Tea-Leaf would have—'

'Tea-Leaf?' said Griffin, looking intrigued. 'I know someone of that name.'

'She knew yours too,' said Hoax. 'She had a guardian, when she was a young kid, who was a real big fan of yours.'

Griffin gave a wry smile.

'Little Tea-Leaf . . .' he murmured. 'She was

always a feisty one, even as an infant. I'm not surprised Salt has found her worthy of your order.'

'Then . . . it was *you* who looked after her?' said Hoax, peering at Griffin searchingly. 'Why didn't you tell her who you really were?'

'It would have put her in great danger,' said Griffin simply. 'Hanging out with a wanted enemy of the Corporation doesn't go down well with the Chairman.'

Hoax grinned.

'Can't wait to see the look on her face when I tell her!'

There was a loud bang and a shower of blue sparks burst from one of the control console's spinning dials. Oddball gave it his immediate attention.

'Don't get your hopes up, Hoax,' he said a few moments later. 'That was the manual control system. Just blew a whole dunk-load of fuses. Until I fix it, the ship is stuck on the course I set.'

He peered out of the cockpit's patched view-shield. The wall of crackling green energy ahead was fast approaching. 'And from where I'm sitting, that containment field still looks one hundred per cent intact.'

He looked up at Hoax.

'Unless Rake knocks that thing out in the next ninety seconds, it's a fair bet you won't be seeing Tea-Leaf – or anyone else for that matter – anytime soon!'

Chapter 15
Breakthrough

In the West One Peace Keep, the Chairman was enjoying his last few moments gloating over Griffin's hopeless predicament. Any time now, Decimal would give the order for the White Knights to advance. The fun wouldn't last long after that. It was almost a shame.

As he looked across the holographic battle-zone map again, delighting in the way the mass of troops symbolized his power, a glint of silvery-grey caught his eye.

'What's that?'

He batted General Decimal on the shoulder and pointed.

'Look – there!'

Something was moving across the centre of the map. It hadn't been there a moment ago. It had appeared just above the ruined reactor building.

Decimal immediately ordered one of his officers to provide a visual close-up. A video image flashed up moments later on the control room's main display. What it showed was quite bizarre.

'What on Jupiter's moons is *that*?' said the Chairman.

It looked like someone had taken a massive piece of rusted metal, magnetized it so that hundreds of other bits of scrap had stuck randomly to it, then somehow got the whole lot airborne.

'I believe it's some kind of ship,' replied Decimal.

The Chairman's eyes flashed. 'Griffin!' he hissed.

Decimal looked back anxiously at the battle-zone map. The mystery craft was moving due east, surprisingly fast.

The Chairman was tracking its course too.

'It's heading straight towards us!'

Decimal frowned.

'It will strike the containment field first,' he said. 'They'll burn up as soon as they hit it.

Why would they want to do that?'

'Maybe it's some sort of trick,' said the Chairman. 'Maybe there's nobody on board.'

He was becoming increasingly agitated. He was not going to let Griffin slip through his fingers again.

'Send your troops in now!' he barked at Decimal. 'That thing has to be a diversion. Look at it – it's not fit to be manned. Our knights will finish those Skirter scum on the ground!'

But Decimal was lost in thought. He already knew from the scanner data being fed directly into his brain that there *were* people on board the strange ship. For them to fly into the field was suicide. It made no sense. He didn't like things that didn't make sense. To Decimal, logic was everything.

'The only way it could work as an escape strategy,' he murmured to himself, 'is if somehow . . .'

His computer-aided brain finally solved the puzzle.

'The field generator!'

He whirled round urgently to address his chief officer.

'Check the status of all the field generator's systems, immediately!'

But even as he yelled his orders, an electronic siren broke into a loud wail. All across the control room, alarm lights began flashing red.

Decimal turned back to the holographic map. Before his horrified gaze, a triangular section of the containment field fizzled, then blinked out. The failed zone lay directly in the flight-path of the Skirter ship.

The Chairman, beside him, was turning purple. He began screaming like a lunatic, to anyone who would listen.

'ATTACK! ATTACK! ALL UNITS ADVANCE IMMEDIATELY! DON'T LET THEM GET AWAY!'

Salt swung the nose of the *Sieger* out of the docking bay and began to steer her towards the exit of the Peace Keep's shuttle garage.

For once, the old Armouron was uncertain what his next step should be. He had delivered Lanista's repaired armour only so he could get closer to the scene of his team's secret activities – because he feared they weren't secret any more.

Lanista's search of the sewers suggested she was on to Oddball and Hoax, at least. Salt had fully expected to arrive at the Keep to hear news of their capture. He had spent the journey from the Academy trying – without success – to think of a way to get them out of trouble.

But his worries had been unnecessary. The Corporation assistant to whom he had delivered the spaulders had been adamant. Lanista was not at the Keep. Nor had there been any recent news from or about her.

Salt knew that no news was definitely good news. Maybe Oddball and Hoax had managed to escape the Chairman's sister somehow.

But it left him with the problem of what to do now. To choose how best to help his students, he needed to know how the mission was going.

He didn't have to wait long. As the *Sieger* glided out from the mouth of the garage, Salt looked west towards the glowing dome of the containment field – and his heart soared.

In the near face of the dome, a triangular window of clear sky was plainly visible.

An instant later, a large, oddly-shaped aircraft burst through it. It zoomed straight towards the Peace Keep, thundered narrowly past its battlements and roared away eastwards across the sky.

They did it! Thank the Twelve!

Salt no longer needed telling what to do. His young knights had got Griffin out, it was clear. Now he had to get them home safely.

The original plan had been for the two teams to meet up after the mission at a specified sewer airshaft. They could then return to the Old School the way Oddball and Hoax had left, through the disused tunnels.

But that's no good now, thought Salt anxiously. *The Corporation is on to the fact that someone is using the sewers. They're not safe.*

He would have to stop the young Armouron trying to get back that way. As the rendezvous was on his way back to Nu-Topia, he could fly the *Sieger* there. If he managed to intercept Rake and the others, he could transport them to the Academy in the shuttle. It would be simple enough for them to then sneak back into the Old School via the secret passage from the garage. They could resume their 'punishment' duties without anyone being any the wiser.

The key was to catch them in time.

Salt pulled the *Sieger* round in a tight curve, until she was pointing east. He fired up the main thrusters and opened their throttles out to full.

Chapter 16
Regrets and Reconciliations

'I would have liked to have seen him again,' said Tea-Leaf quietly.

Through one of the *Sieger*'s side windows, she watched the dark speck retreating into the blue sky. The *Inimitable* was rapidly leaving Nu-Topia's airspace, heading east.

She turned away, a wistful look in her eyes, and began removing her breastplate. Her four cadet friends were a little ahead of her. They were already stowing their armour in the shuttle's secret storage hold.

'He would have stuck around if he could,' said Oddball. 'But by the time I'd managed to get that rust-bucket's manual controls working again, and

Tock and I had talked Griffin through how to fly her so that he could drop us off, they couldn't hang about.'

Hoax stashed his last piece of yellow armour, then turned and nodded his agreement.

'It won't take long for Decimal to organize a pursuit,' he said. 'Griffin wanted to get well clear before there are Kettle fighters all over his tail.'

Tea-Leaf knew they were right, but she was still bitterly disappointed. She, Snow and Rake had arrived at the rendezvous only minutes after Hoax and Oddball, to see the *Inimitable* heading off into the distance. She had been amazed to hear that her much-loved former guardian was on board the fleeing vessel. Salt had arrived in the *Sieger* moments later, just in time to pick up his team before they set off down into the sewer tunnels.

Tea-Leaf removed her remaining armour in silence. Once it was safely hidden, she moved to the window once more. The Skirters' ramshackle ship had now completely disappeared from view.

'Where do you think he'll go?'

'Dunno for sure,' said Hoax. 'Somewhere he and the other Skirters can set up without the Corporation breathing down their necks, I guess. They'll lie low for a while, regroup, then – who knows? I seriously doubt we've seen the last of him . . .'

Rake approached Salt, who sat silently at the shuttle's flight controls. The old armourer had said little since picking them up.

'Master?'

'Yes, Templer?'

'I've been thinking. Griffin has an obvious gift for leadership. He's a superb warrior – your top student, you said. And he clearly hates the

Corporation. So why didn't you ever enrol him as an Armouron knight?'

Salt gave an indignant grunt.

'Don't think I never thought of doing so!' he rumbled. 'But back in the days when Griffin was at the Academy, I was in no position to recruit anyone. I had the five medallions in my possession, yes. But I lacked the means or materials to craft such suits as you now possess.'

He turned to look at Rake gravely.

'Besides, not all great champions are destined to bear a medallion. An Armouron Knight must serve as one member of a unified team. Griffin was – and still is – a courageous and noble-minded individual. But he is just that – an individual, a lone operator. There was always something a little . . . *reckless* about the boy.'

His steely gaze shifted from Rake to Tea-Leaf.

'In that respect, he is not unlike another of my pupils . . .'

Tea-Leaf braced herself. She was only too aware that having stormed off from the mission briefing, then followed her own plan of action, she was bound to be in big trouble.

But before Salt could launch into the lecture he

clearly had planned, Rake cut in.

'Master . . .' He hesitated, a little red in the face, as though what he was about to say didn't come easily. 'Before you give Tea-Leaf a hard time, you should know that if it wasn't for her, the mission would have been a disaster.'

Tea-Leaf was gobsmacked. Her number one critic was coming to her defence.

'I was all set to blow the containment field sky-high until she showed up,' Rake continued. 'That would have done for everyone. It was only because she cracked the generator's control systems that we got the field down at all. She saved my skin too. And Snow's.'

Salt frowned.

'That may be so, but it does not excuse her earlier actions. Going off on her own like that put us all at risk.'

Rake wasn't finished.

'But that was only because I objected to having her on the team.' He looked down awkwardly. 'I shouldn't have. We need her, just as much as anyone else.'

It was Tea-Leaf's turn to blush a little. Snow gave her a warm grin.

Salt studied Rake silently, still scowling. But he said nothing further and a small smile crept across his lips. The young Armouron were beginning to stand together as a real team and he was quietly pleased. He gave another grunt, turned back to the *Sieger*'s controls and dipped the shuttle's nose towards the Academy, the Old School and home.

Rake turned. 'Stand Together . . .' he said softly.

'Battle as One,' Tea-Leaf whispered back.

They grinned at each other.

Chapter 17
In the Rubble

Back in the control room of the West One Peace Keep, the Chairman and his Chief of Peace were still watching the main display. It now showed the image from the helmet-cam of one of the first wave of White Knights to reach the reactor.

There was almost nothing of the power station left standing. The *Inimitable*'s earth-shaking engines had brought most of its remaining walls crashing down during her lift-off. The whole area was a sea of rubble. And so far there had been no sign of a single Skirter.

As the White Knight wearing the helmet-cam picked its way through the ruins, the Chairman suddenly caught sight of something sticking out of a pile of collapsed masonry.

'What's that?'

General Decimal ordered the android camera man to zoom in.

It was a hand.

Within minutes, the White Knights had cleared away enough rubble to reveal the dust-covered body of a woman. As they removed yet more debris, she began to stir. Her eyes suddenly opened, flashing with anger. She lashed out with one leg and began yelling a steady stream of colourful curses.

The Chairman turned slowly to his military commander, who was staring in disbelief at the video display.

'General.' There was a trace of menace behind the Corporation leader's soft tone. 'What is my sister doing at the centre of your battle-zone?'

Decimal didn't reply. Despite his exceptional intelligence and all the computer chips implanted in his brain, he really couldn't come up with an answer.

If you enjoyed *The Caged Griffin*,
you might like a sneak preview of the next book
in the series: *Prisoner on Kasteesh*.
Turn over for the first few pages . . .

PRISONER ON KASTEESH

Richard Dungworth

A BANTAM BOOK 978 0 553 82197 0
Copyright © RDF Media Ltd/Armouron L td, 2010

Chapter 1
The Voice

Snow tried to calm her mind and focus. *Panic is your greatest enemy.* That was what Salt had told them. *Fear only clouds your senses.*

She kept her eyes fixed on the strange mechanical device hovering at eye level a few metres away. It was gunmetal-grey and the size and shape of a handball. It was moving erratically – left, right, up, down – kept airborne by a whirring rotor. Its lower surface bristled with tubular silver spines. She had no idea which of them would shoot. She was on the balls of her feet, knees slightly bent, ready to dodge.

There was a sudden *pfft* of escaping air. Snow threw herself into a dive to her left. Something fizzed past her to ricochet off the stone floor, kicking up a little puff of dust.

Snow used the momentum of her dive to roll through and spring back onto her feet. When the device fired its second shot an instant later, she was ready.

This time she sensed its aim was low. She launched herself into a high tuck-jump and another tiny projectile whistled past under her feet.

She landed lightly – in time to hear the device let out a third soft hiss. Snow ducked urgently to the right. But she was a fraction too slow.

There was a metallic *ping!* and Snow felt something glance off her armoured shoulder.

'Gotcha!'

Oddball stepped forward, grinning. He strode towards the spiky flying device. As it continued to dart about, he reached up to slap a switch on its underside. The machine's rotor immediately began to slow and it drifted lower. Oddball plucked it from the air. He turned to Snow, eyes sparkling behind his ever-present goggles.

'Two out of three – pretty impressive for a practice run!' he congratulated her.

He held up the peculiar flying device proudly.

'What do you make of it?'

Before Snow could answer, he went gabbling on.

'I thought I might call it the "PShooter". "P" for "pressure", you see, 'cos it runs entirely on compressed air. You just have to pump it up. The air chamber holds enough to power it for a couple of minutes. The shooter-tubes work off the same pressurized system. It's totally random which ones fire, of course – that's what keeps you on your toes!'

He gripped the gadget between his knees, produced a miniature hand pump and began energetically pumping air into a valve in the device's side.

'Salt asked me to put together something to help improve our reflexes. I thought this might do the job. I pinched the fan for the rotor from one of the big dryers in the laundry. The rest is just bits and bobs I found lying around.'

Snow watched him pumping away enthusiastically and smiled to herself. Every good team needed a techno-geek. Of the group of recently recruited Armouron Knights, Oddball was certainly that guy. Salt couldn't have found a more gadget-mad individual in the whole of the Academy – or Nu-Topia, for that matter.

He must have had his reasons to choose each of us, I guess, thought Snow.

It was several months now since Salt, the Academy's elderly armourer, had introduced Snow and her three fellow cadets – Oddball, Rake and Hoax – to an exciting new world of adventure and danger.

🏵 ⅋ 🜂 ⬢ 🏵 🅐 🜂 ⬡ ⬤ ✪

Up until then, their lives had been just like those of the other orphans raised at the Academy. Day in, day out, they had pursued their Gladiator training in preparation for their future careers in the Arena, where they would fight staged battles for the entertainment of Nu-Topia's citizens. They had been confined at all times to the Academy compound, kept within its walls like prisoners.

But not any more. Now, they lived double-lives. During the daytime, they continued as before, regular Academy cadets, attending their lessons and carrying out their chores. But by night, wearing the unique suits of armour that Salt had crafted for them, they became Alida, Sappar, Templer and False-Light, knights of the ancient order of the Armouron.

Salt had opened their eyes to the corruption in the world around them – the so-called 'Perfect World', as its unscrupulous ruler, the Chairman, called it. The Chairman had used his influence as leader of the all-powerful Corporation to brain-wash the citizens of Earth into believing his lies. Those who didn't were soon silenced by his sinister police force, the White Knights.

But under Salt's direction, Snow and her fellow

knights were fighting back – fighting to restore the ideals of their order: Honour, Duty, Compassion and Justice.

Not that they were in action every night. Most nights, like tonight, it was training. And more training. And then more training. Salt was a hard taskmaster. As an Armouron himself, he knew the value of being in peak physical and mental condition. He insisted that his young recruits were thoroughly drilled in the techniques and strategies of combat. Each night, down in the secret chambers of the Old School, beneath the Academy, he put them through their paces.

So far tonight, though, only Snow and Oddball were there for training.

They hadn't been expecting Tea-Leaf, the fifth member of the team. Unlike the others, Tea-Leaf wasn't an Academy cadet, but lived outside the compound, on the city streets. Her only route into the Old School was via a secret passage from the Academy's shuttle garage. Salt had heard news that the garage was to be under close police guard over the next few days. If White Knights were patrolling the area, it was better that Tea-Leaf stay well clear. During the previous night's session, he had warned her to stay away.

So a no-show from Tea-Leaf was no surprise. But Salt wasn't impressed when neither Hoax nor Rake turned up, either – even less so when Oddball confessed he had heard a rumour that the other boys were in a 'spot of bother'.

Salt had given a weary sigh, then departed to find out more – but not before instructing Oddball and Snow to work on their reaction times while he was gone.

Oddball suddenly detached the pump and pulled the PShooter from between his knees.

'That should do it!'

He lifted a flap in the gadget's casing, emptied a handful of small ball-bearings into it, then closed the flap again.

'OK – so this time is for real. Fully charged, she'll fire eight shots. We'll score how many you dodge. Rake managed five last night – that's the best so far.'

Rake would like that, thought Snow. It was pretty important to Rake to be the best at things. He liked to be in charge too. It didn't bother Snow – Rake made a pretty natural team-leader. But she knew it got on Hoax's nerves sometimes. Tea-

Leaf, too, didn't always take kindly to being told what to do.

'Are you ready?' asked Oddball, preparing to launch the PShooter.

But before Snow's trial could begin, a burly figure came limping along the passageway that led to the secret doorway back into the armoury. It was Salt. His expression was even more gruff than usual.

'What's he done this time, master?' asked Oddball. Hoax had a well-deserved reputation for mischief.

Salt gave a grunt of exasperation.

'Your young friend was apparently responsible for this evening's security alarm,' he growled. 'He seems to have believed – foolishly – that it would be amusing to stage a fake cadet breakout. From what I can gather, he got hold of a spare identity belt, yet to be registered, and put it down the canteen rubbish chute. When the refuse collection vehicle picked up the Academy's waste just after lights-out, it took the belt with it. Naturally, it triggered the security systems as it left the compound.'

Oddball tried to hide his smirk. 'And they

managed to pin it on Hoax, did they?' he said. 'It's not like him to get caught.'

'By all accounts, he was unable to contain his delight when his childish prank proved a success,' Salt explained, stony-faced. 'Supervisor Brand deduced from his mirth that he was responsible – despite Rake protesting there was no proof. Rake should have known better. Brand has given them both an overnight punishment detail.'

The old man suddenly clapped his bear-sized hands together.

'But enough of their foolishness! Let's get back to work!' He turned to Snow. 'How are those reaction times coming on, Alida?' he asked, using Snow's secret Armouron name.

'She's good,' answered Oddball on Snow's behalf. 'Really good. You should see some of her dodge moves!'

'I'm glad to hear it,' rumbled Salt. 'The armour I crafted for you, Alida, was specifically designed to enhance your natural agility. Only Balista's suit is lighter. It should allow you ease of movement, at all times.'

It was true. Snow still found it amazing that wearing her blue armour made her *more* agile, not less. Any ordinary suit would have slowed you down. But there was nothing ordinary about the suits Salt had made for them.

'And remember,' continued Salt, 'your armour's evasive properties will be maximized only if you harness the power of your medallion. Connect to its Flow and your agility will be greatly increased.'

Snow raised a hand over her Armouron medallion, embedded in her breastplate, and nodded silently.

That concluded Salt's pep talk. He took a few steps backwards, to give Snow some space.

'Whenever you're ready then, Alida. Let's see what you can do.'

As Oddball got ready once more to release the PShooter, Snow prepared herself again, up on her toes, mind fully focused.

The device whirred into the air and immediately began darting from side to side.

Its first shot was aimed low, at Snow's legs. Snow side-stepped it easily. As the device released its next two missiles, almost simultaneously, she cartwheeled to the left. Both ball-bearings whistled harmlessly past. A swift dive and roll enabled her to dodge shots four and five. She was back on her feet in time to evade the device's next effort, then jump high to avoid another low-flying shot.

Eight shots, Oddball had said. That left just one more.

Suddenly, Snow's concentration was shattered by a nerve-splitting scream of anguish, which exploded in her mind.

She dropped helplessly to her knees and began clawing at her helmet clasp, as though releasing it might somehow let the agonizing yell out of her head.

TAKE THE ARMOURON CHALLENGE!

A new generation of brave and
loyal knights are needed to join
the battle against the Perfect Corporation
and bring justice back to the galaxy.

Have you got what it takes?

If you think you could be
an Armouron knight, head to
www.armouronbooks.co.uk to find out!

STAND TOGETHER ...
BATTLE AS ONE!